Estella of Halftree Village

A Sasquatch Tale

Rachel Westfall

&

Ursula Westfall

CONTENTS

1. The sweet burden of berries

This was a day for gathering berries. The sun rose golden on the hills, illuminating the rich, red fruit strewn over the forest floor. Elena and I set out early, bare feet padding down the cool trail, birch bark baskets tucked under our arms and balanced on our hips. The boys would join us if they could, but they had been called away to the fish camp today.

Elena danced ahead, laughing. "Estella," she called, "let's find our fortunes in the stream!" "Wait for me," I called after her, stepping gingerly along the stony path to the creek.

I found her at the water, the little creek bumbling and murmuring its way through the pebbled causeway. This spot had been special to us since we were little girls. Most of the stones were ordinary, but to a sharp eye, it was a treasure trove of geodes and glowing golden agates. Each one, we whispered and giggled to one another a lifetime ago, held a tiny vision of the future. Choose the right stone, and a girl could find the image of her beloved.

I hiked up my skirts and followed Elena hesitantly into the creek. The cool water sent a shiver through me, and my feet were soon numb. Elena had already plunged in up to her calves, the water swirling around her legs as she searched through the stones at the creek-bottom, digging for her fortune. Her basket lay forgotten at the creek side, and I had nestled mine inside it.

Elena looked up at me, grinning. The ends of her long, dark hair dripped with creek water, and she held up a milky agate, lobed, as large as a fist. I grinned back and began to dig for my own treasure. Elena made her way to the shore and sat on a large, flat stone to read her fortune.

"I see a face. This is my best stone yet!"

"What does the face look like?" I continued rooting around on the creek-bottom, but I had stirred up a lot of silt, clouding the water. The chill had crept up to my knees. I gave up and pulled myself out of the creek, up onto the rock beside Elena.

She held up the stone; the morning sun behind it made me wince. I took it and shaded it with my hand. Yes, there was a shape inside. Was it a face?

"What do you think?" Elena chirped, "Could it be him?" Elena had a huge crush on one of the young men from the village. Ethan was a burly, well-muscled youth, good-natured and kind. "It could be," I teased. "It's shaped like his muscly chest." Elena smacked me on the shoulder, and I jumped back into the water, laughing. I splashed her and she shrieked.

"Watch it!" Nana stood at the creek side, scowling down at us.

Our faces fell. I must have splashed her by accident, as she was wiping creek water off her stern brow.

"Sorry Nana," "Just washing off our feet, Nana," we mumbled, snatching up our berry baskets. Nana held out a little packet of flatbread wrapped in a broadleaf. I took it, kissing her dry cheek lightly, then Elena and I scurried off to find the nearest berry patch.

☼

Saska peeped around a fallen log and watched the girls leave. He ducked back quickly as the one called Nana looked his way, her expression sharp. She stood still for several moments, humming softly to herself. Then she turned and shuffled back down the path.

Those girls. One in particular had caught his attention, his breath catching in his throat as he thought of her. Quickly and silently, he traced her route through the woods. He had seen a few humans in his time, but never one as pretty and fiery as this one. Never had he seen the colour of her hair on anyone else, deep ebony black. It looked, he decided, almost as dark and shiny as a bird's beady eye.

He mouthed her name. Estella.

I will leave something for her, he thought. *Something that's special.*

Saska lumbered off into the bushes, looking for the most delicious berry he could find. After much searching and taste-testing, he found an extremely ripe raspberry, squishy and dark red, almost violet in the morning sun's light. It was the tail end of the season for raspberries, and they were at their sweetest. *It's perfect,* he thought. He picked it gingerly off the bush and placed it on an old log near the trail leading to the creek. Beside it, he set a well-ripened, dried fish that he had been planning to eat later.

A rustling noise near the creek alerted him. He cocked his woolly head a little to the side and held still. Rabbits? He heard the sound again, but this time it was accompanied by a voice. "Be quiet! Do you want him to hear us!?" the voice hissed.

Saska could smell the humans now, their city scent fouling the breeze. He wished he could make a stew out of them, but he knew that was a terrible idea, as it would draw the attention of more humans. People randomly disappearing in the woods? *Yeah, that no be suspicious at all,* he thought sarcastically.

Saska retreated through the bushes to his cave, making sure to cover up his tracks thoroughly. "Find him, you fools!" a young man screamed. "I'm sure I saw him just now. He can't have gone far!"

The humans stomped about in their shiny boots and smacked the bushes with their polished walking sticks, determined to find evidence of some kind. One of them, wearing a dapper button-shirt and pressed khaki pants, pulled a pair of polished binoculars from his pack and scanned the horizon. He squinted and rubbed his eyes, to no avail.

Saska knew they had lost his trail when he heard their angry mutters and curses fade away in the distance. He sighed in relief, scratching his brown, hairy feet. He munched on a few of the nuts that he'd stashed in his cave, then dug around in the moist dirt floor, finding several plump worms. He popped them into his mouth and chewed happily.

☼

Kurt scratched the bug bites on his neck and shoulder as he scanned the area, looking for clues. He put away the binoculars; dratted things were useless in the bush, anyway. All he could see were trees and more trees, and the sounds of the forest were creeping him out. He and the boys were horribly intimidated by their boss, and though they were working independently for now, their boss would be joining them at Halftree village in a few days. Kurt quietly cursed the man under his breath, then spat to the side.

Kurt and the boys needed the work, so this was how they had to live, because good paying jobs were rare in the city. It was this or running drugs, or worse. All the old family money had dried up generations ago, and there wasn't much else out there for city boys without a lot of book-learning. Kurt was lucky his father had some success in the tech industry. He was better off than most.

"Kurt?" It was the boys, back from their scrounging in the dirt. The little one, the one he called Ferret on account of his weasel face, had a steadily dripping nose. He dabbed at it now with his grubby sleeve. He held up a small brown tuft of hair which he'd found hanging from a twig.

"Is this what we're looking for?"

Kurt raised an eyebrow at Ferret, then popped the bit of fluff into a baggie and pocketed it.

The other boy was a big lug who everyone called Runt. He had a round, open face that tended to flush red, and his hair danced with unruly waves and curls. Runt had picked up a sack of some sort in the village, and he was swinging it around now pathetically, trying to keep the bugs off him, sending dust flying.

"Can we get out of here now, Kurt? There's nothing here, and I'm getting hungry."

Kurt pulled out his eWare and tapped a quick micro.

GoldenBoy23 / Halftree backwoods, hunting for fluff #bestjjobever/

Someone in the village had tipped them off about the sasquatch; if they could capture one, they could feed their families for years on the earnings. There were still plenty of rich old farts in the city who were dying to add to their collections of endangered species. They'd probably tear each other apart arguing over who'd get to keep this one. *Gum each other to death, more likely*, he thought, chuckling.

Though he was pretty sure they were on the right track, he wasn't too confident about the information they got from their village tipster. They had chosen the young man almost at random and asked him what he knew about sasquatches. The fellow had seemed genuine enough, though a bit dense. He was a big fellow, slow to speak, but happy to point them in the right direction with the promise of a "reward."

He'll get his rewards, all right, Kurt thought. Had he been trying to mislead them? He had said that sasquatches were calm and friendly, and they had dark green hair that helped them blend in with their habitat. Suspiciously, the tuft of hair they had just found was dark brown. They'd have to shake the fella up a bit when they got back to the village, just to show him who was boss.

☼

I brushed the crumbs from my mouth and grinned at Elena as we finished downing the baked flatbread that Nana had given us. Our baskets were piled with ripe berries, and the sun was low in the sky now. It was time to start heading back.

"Let's go!" Elena chirped, jumping to her feet. She always was the hyper one. I stood, groaning, and brushed the flakes of dried leaves and remnants of our dinner from my skirt. We scooped up our baskets and headed for the creek.

As usual, Elena got there ahead of me. I took my time, picking a few mushrooms along the way, adding them to the berry harvest. If we didn't eat them tonight, we would dry them, and they would help keep us fed through the long winter.

At the creek, Elena already had her feet wet. "Where did my rock go? I'm sure I put it over here when Nana caught us earlier." I scanned around, but in the falling light, I couldn't see her special rock. That was the problem with rocks. In amongst the others, they all looked the same to me. Elena was so much better at finding the good ones than I was.

Something gleamed pearl-like in the water. Puzzled, I reached in and drew it out. Drying it on my shirt, I saw that I had found a rare white agate, its hue making me think of the moon. Quietly, I held it out to Elena.

"What have you got there?" she snapped. "That's not my rock!"

"It's a new one, maybe a special one." I breathed on it and looked inside. Could I see something…. hairy? Elena peered over my shoulder at it. "It's all woolly inside, like Uncle John's butt!" she laughed. I scowled and swatted at her, grinning. She swatted back, and soon we were wrestling in the water, laughing.

A stick cracked nearby, and we both jumped.

"Did you hear something?"

"Shh, listen."

The faint sound of voices came to us on the breeze. We heard a sharp tone, like someone cursing. "It sounds like those annoying boys. Let's go," I said.

We grabbed our baskets and headed up to the trail. As I stepped over a log, I noticed an odd smell. It was like a cross between fish and old socks. Was that seriously a fish lying across the log, dead as can be? Yes, definitely a fish. It smelled as if it had been out of the water for some time.

Elena wrinkled her nose. "What's that smell? It smells like our old grandpa."

I snorted. Grandpa always smelled of old fish, since he was in charge of the fish camp. He'd be up to his armpits in fish guts at this very moment. We were lucky to be picking berries instead of gutting fish!

But what was that beside the very dead fish? It looked like a ripe raspberry. Where had it come from? Had it fallen from one of our baskets? I reached out to pinch it between my fingers, but it fell apart like jam.

"Eww," I moaned, disgusted. "I hate squishy berries!" I rubbed my soiled fingers on the edge of my damp skirt.

I stepped gingerly over the fish, thinking an eagle or bear must have left it there. Or maybe a squirrel. I saw one once, dragging a fish larger than its own body through the woods. You never know what squirrels will take! Or boys. They will pick up anything, too. Maybe one of the village boys had put the fish there, wanting to prank us.

We ran all the way to the village, our baskets balanced carefully on our hips, if only to get home ahead of the boys.

In his cavern, Saska settled down on his haunches, thinking about the human girls and grooming himself. He had been pretty lonely since he parted from his mother and grandfather last spring. Sasquatches are very solitary beings. It was customary for someone his age to head out and find a backwoods squat of his own, but he hadn't quite gotten used to it yet.

He wasn't sure how he felt about meeting Estella in person. Meeting with any human was incredibly dangerous, he'd been told. Any direct contact was probably ill-advised.

He thought about it while scratching his head. He pulled something from his scalp, inspected it and crushed it between two fingernails. He absentmindedly popped it into his mouth as he thought about what his grandfather had told him, years ago.

Don't ever fall in love with a human… or it may end in tragedy.

2. By the light of the harvest moon

As we approached the village, Elena slowed and held out an arm to stop me. "Shh, listen."

Frowning, I heard the low voices of men, women and children going about the preparations for the evening meal. Several large bonfires blazed at the centre of the village, as was the nightly tradition at this time of year. Together, we would feast on the seasonal bounty: fish, berries, and plump wild tubers. The food would be flavoured with wild herbs and a few traditional spices, grown in the kitchen gardens of the elders.

We heard Ethan's cheerful laugh, and several of the village boys trotted past the fire with armloads of wood for burning.

"How did they get ahead of us?" Elena gave me a puzzled look and shrugged, her brow furrowed.

We set our baskets down beside Nana, who sat before a row of fresh fish, wrapping them in broad leaves for steaming. She patted the ground beside her, and we settled down to help her. It was quite dark now, and fireflies blinked lazily by.

"Did you see anything unusual out there today?" she asked.

"Well, we could hear the boys, but somehow they got here ahead of us. And there were bear tracks on the berry trail."

Nana shook her head. "The boys weren't out that way today. They were at the fish camp all day. There were some city boys snooping around earlier though. They wanted to know if we'd seen any unusual wildlife."

"Like what?" We had all the usual wildlife here: bears, birds, moose....

Nana just shrugged. "Something from the old stories, I suppose."

"Tell us a story, Nana," Elena begged. I nodded hopefully. Nana told the best stories!

"After dinner, girls, after dinner." Nana always said we'd get more patient as we got older, but I wondered when that patience was supposed to magically appear. It clearly hadn't happened yet.

Elena and I shared an irritated glance, then she elbowed me softly. I looked up and saw Ethan approaching. He nodded to me and Nana in greeting, and his eyes lit up for Elena.

"Hi Elena," he said, blushing slightly. "Want to see what I made today?" She nodded, and he held out his hand. Nestled in it was a little wooden carving of a bear, cleverly made. Ethan was remarkably skilled with his hands.

"So that's what you were doing when the other boys were working, eh?" Nana scolded.

Ethan's face fell. "I gutted plenty of fish first." Nana huffed, but she said nothing more.

"I think it's very sweet," Elena quickly said. "Right, Estella?" I nodded encouragingly.

Ethan's smile lit up his face again. He handed the little carving to Elena, then ran back to join the boys. She toyed with it, running it over her hands.

"Ask that one what he told the city boys today," Nana grumbled. I raised an eyebrow at Elena, but she just shrugged.

After we shared a delicious, fire-roasted meal, Nana was true to her word. The harvest moon rose, huge and golden, as she settled back into her familiar story-teller's pose. A circle of young and old villagers drew in close, sitting tightly and quietly in anticipation. A few little ones sat in the adults' laps. Everyone loved hearing Nana tell stories. I closed my eyes, settled against Elena's shoulder, and waited for my imagination to follow Nana into her story.

It all began on a warm day in late summer, not so unlike this day ....

☼

Halftree Village was new, then. A handful of families had built it to make a fresh start. They had run from the city life, where gang warfare and corruption had reached an all-time high. Back-to-the-landers, people called them; villages were popping up in the woods like mushrooms. With rampant poverty, violence and disease in the cities, it was no wonder that so many people were willing to walk away from it all and start over, leaving behind the more advanced urban technologies.

I was young then, as young as my granddaughters are now, and I was full of the wild energy of youth. My job was to pick berries, as many as I could. It was soon to be our third winter here and we'd need all the food we could store to feed all the villagers until spring. Scrounging for food in the wilds wasn't that different from rooting in the dumpsters for food in the cities, like so many kids did to survive, but without the gangs, or the danger of infection from stepping on a filthy bit of wire. But that's a story for another day.

I winded my way down the trail to the creek, the very same creek that runs near the village here today, and empties its waters into Fish Lake. I stopped to wash my face in the water. As I turned around, I thought I saw something move, just at the corner of my vision. A closer look revealed nothing out of place. I picked up my basket and headed back towards my favourite berry patch, stepping over a fallen log. The trail wasn't very good then.

I spent the whole day out there picking berries. When I got hungry, I picked a few for my stomach. When I got thirsty, I went back down to the creek and scooped up some water, using my hands as a dish.

The second time I went to the creek, it was early evening, and the sun cast long, low tracks of brilliance through the trees. The rays blinded me such that I almost missed it: a dead fish, stretched out flat over a fallen log. I'd crossed that log several times now, and I swear that fish wasn't there before. Good scavenger that I was, I picked up the fish, wrapped it in leaves, and added it to the berry basket. We ate well that night.

Where does a fish come from in the woods, you might ask? Well, fresh from the city, I knew enough not to look a gift horse in the mouth. I suppose I might have thought an eagle left it there, or a bear. Even a cheeky squirrel. But I thought none of those things. All I thought about was my stomach!

Well, the next day, I went out to pick berries again. Lo and behold, there on that same log, what did I find? A mushroom. Beautiful, ripe and plump. I grinned, thinking for sure that I'd hit pay dirt, like this was some kind of magic log or something. I popped the mushroom into my basket, thinking no more of it.

By the third day, I actually started to wonder who was putting such delicious foods on that log. Where were they, and why did they let me take the food away? Wouldn't a wild animal guard his food stash?

I put a small pile of pine nuts on the log, then I went down to the creek and hunkered down behind a rock to watch and wait. After a few minutes, sure enough, I could hear something coming through the bushes. It was definitely much too large to be a squirrel. A bear, maybe? Or a clumsy raccoon?

My eyes grew wide as I saw a furry hand slowly reach up around the log.

The hand grasped the seeds in fingers not unlike yours or mine, then another hand slid up and placed something on the log. I couldn't see what it was from this angle, but I was frozen in place. I wondered if I had hallucinated the whole thing. I rubbed my eyes.

Twigs cracking in the distance let me know the creature was gone. Looking around furtively, I crept back over to the log to discover a little pile of juicy, ripe berries. Hesitantly, I picked one up. It looked delicious. I sniffed it, then popped it in my mouth.

We didn't have a name for such creatures yet, but I believe to this day that my new secret friend was what we now call a bushman or a sasquatch.

Maybe it's true, and maybe it's not. You can choose for yourselves what you wish to believe.

☼

"What happened to him, Nana? Where did he go?" one of the little ones asked.

Nana's face darkened. "Men from the city came looking for him. Bounty hunters. But that, too, is a story for another day."

As Nana finished telling her story, I opened my eyes and looked around. That was when I noticed three strangers leaning against the wooden siding of a nearby hut. One was a big galoot carrying a large backpack; he fussed unhappily with his cowlicky hair. The second fellow had a narrow face and large teeth. He shifted and twitched from side to side as if he itched all over. The third wore a dapper button shirt and khaki pants. His short hair was slicked back, and his sharp eyes were narrowed. He stroked his goatee thoughtfully, looking intently at Nana.

3. To snare a sasquatch

Saska peered suspiciously out of his cave. Nothing moved. He snuck out and ducked quickly behind a tree, scanning the horizon through a veil of leaves. The morning autumn sun was the only thing that moved. He sighed in relief and sat down on a log.

He heard an angry buzz, followed by a painful jab. He leaped up, yelping, "Me buttock! Me poor tender buttock!"

He spun around and came face-to-face with a giant wasp. He had never seen such a creature in all of his life. It was as big as the palm of his hand, shiny black, and clearly displeased about having been sat upon. The wasp buzzed angrily, brandishing its stinger.

Saska ran away, alarmed, the wasp chasing after him. As he ran, he almost cracked his head on a birch wood box which dangled from a tree by a rope. Its lid was open. He could smell a city boy's stench on it now.

Is that where the wasp had come from? How else would a random giant wasp appear out of midair? But what was the purpose of it?

As he ran by, the wasp buzzing behind him hotly, he spotted something out of place under a clump of bushes. A human laid there, draped in red and burnt-orange clothing. The human's muffled snores were audible over the angry wasp's buzzing. A waft of city-stench drifted over.

He darted up a hill, feinting right then diving to the left into a thicket of brambles. The wasp continued on, buzzing ferociously. He rubbed his tender buttock, wincing at the pain and fingering the huge welt that the stinger had left. He felt so terribly sad, alone and confused. Why would anyone want to hurt him?

☼

Kurt returned from his scouting and found Runt snoring in the bushes, the wasp trap empty, and signs of a scuffle all around. He gave Runt a rough shake. "Wake up, you fool! We've probably lost the sasquatch already!" Slowly, Runt emerged from the bushes on his hands and knees, blinking.

"From now on your new name is Grunt," Kurt hissed. "Now get up, Grunt! Hop to it, or I'll change your name to a cuss word in three seconds."

Grunt quickly got up before his name could get any worse. He looked down, groaning as he realized how grubby he was. He smoothed out his unruly brown hair and tried to dust himself off.

"Forget about your vanity, Grunt," Kurt sneered. "You will lose half your pay if you don't hurry up and look."

Letting Ferret and Runt do the dirty work, Kurt reached into his pocket and dug out his eWare. A friend had fired him a micro.

Sissy_girl @ goldenboy23 / don't get eaten, K? Bring me a souvenir/

He grinned and typed as he watched the boys hustle.

GoldenBoy23 / tranq wasp took the boys for a ride/

☼

Runt scrambled around, looking for any evidence of where the sasquatch had gone. *If there even is a sasquatch,* he grumbled to himself. They had been out here in the bush for three days already, and they still had found no sign of the beast except for that one tuft of hair. He felt hungry, and he wanted a bath. He crawled into nearby bushes, and climbed up trees, but he saw no evidence of any sasquatch.

"Nothing, sir," Runt said.

"'Nothing, sir,'" Kurt mocked. "Well, you'd better find something before the boss shows up, Grunt!" His face was angry and red as he grabbed Runt's collar, giving him a brisk shake. Though Kurt was the smaller of the two, he found Runt easy to intimidate, so he made the most of it.

"Umm… Kurt?" Ferret said from behind.

"What is it, Ferret?" Kurt said, still holding Runt's collar.

"I found the tranquilizer wasp," he said, holding out the birch wood box, which now hummed with a muted angry buzzing. The huge insect was renowned for being able to fell an animal as large as a horse. It ought to knock out a sasquatch, but the tricky part was getting the wasp and the sasquatch together, with the wasp feeling angry enough to sting, without getting stung yourself.

Kurt stared at the box. "Where did you find this?" he asked.

"Not far from here, actually," Ferret answered. "It might be injured. It was limping a little when I found it, and its wings look kinda bent."

Kurt paused for a moment. "Take me there."

"Why?" Ferret asked, rubbing his drippy nose on his sleeve.

"Something happened to this wasp. There might be some clues. Grunt, you carry the wasp."

Runt rolled his eyes and sighed, but he took the box. He was also carrying the pack containing all their supplies. He'd had just about enough of this. When they got back to the village, he'd have to see about finding another job.

☼

It was getting dark by the time they made it back to the village. Almost immediately, they were confronted by a huge man. His large, reddish-brown beard and burly shoulders gave him the look of a bear, and he leaned over them in an intimidating manner.

"What are you city boys doing here anyway?" the man rumbled. "Lost your way?"

"Looking for critters," Ferret muttered, eyes shifting.

"Looking for a new job." Kurt smacked Runt in the stomach and he grunted.

"Shut up, Grunt. I do the talking for this crew. We're looking for sasquatches. Seen any around here?"

The big man eyed the trio suspiciously. "If you know what's good for you, you'll pack up and leave right now. You don't want to meet a sasquatch. Trust me. You three couldn't even hold your own against a baby one." He stalked off, leaving the three youths standing on the main village path.

"Do something useful, you two. Rub your three brain cells together and see if you can't get some more information from these back-woods hicks. I'm going to lie down and relax." Kurt stormed off, leaving Ferret and Runt with the bag of supplies and the limply buzzing wasp box.

The lad they'd spoken to before, Ethan, was sitting on a nearby porch, whittling a piece of wood. Ferret and Runt wandered over. Runt sat down on the edge of the porch, swinging his legs and picking his nose. Ferret scuffed his shoe in the dirt and sniffled.

"What do you boys want?" Ethan asked.

"Just trying to find some interesting critters," Ferret mumbled.

"Looking for a job," Runt said, firmly. "Know of anyone hiring?"

"We don't have much use for jobs or money around here. Everyone chips in, everyone benefits. That's how it works."

Runt and Ferret looked at one another, confused. Then Ferret ventured, "Who was that big hairy guy, anyway? Is it true that sasquatches are mean? I thought you said they were green and gentle."

"That's what we tell all the newcomers," Ethan chuckled. "John thinks we should be up-front with everyone and try to scare them off. He doesn't like the idea of people bothering the wildlife. Come on, you lads look like you could do with some dinner. If you help fillet the fish, you can eat with us."

Runt groaned; he hated handling fish. Ferret twitched his drippy nose and his stomach rumbled. His stomach decided it. They shuffled after the brawny villager, and despite the unpleasant thought of the work to come, even Runt felt a pang of hunger.

It was all worth it to see the look on Kurt's face later that evening when he strolled over to gawk at Runt and Ferret's delicious mounds of food, piled on hand-carved wooden platters. "Where's mine?" he demanded.

"You didn't help out, so you don't get any," Runt mumbled.

"Oh baloney. Give me that, Grunt," Kurt snapped. He snatched Runt's platter and began eating from it hungrily. Runt hung his head. Ferret just turned away and ate as quickly as possible, hoping Kurt didn't steal his food as well.

Kurt heard a grunt behind him, and he looked over. The big man, John, was scowling down at him. "Is there some trouble over here?"

Kurt ducked his head, just a little. "No trouble, sir. Just having a bite to eat."

"Well, good. Cause we don't like trouble around here. We don't like it one bit."

He lumbered off, Kurt staring daggers at his back. Runt took advantage of Kurt's distraction to snatch a strip of fish off the plate in Kurt's hands. He stuffed it quickly into his mouth. Kurt's narrowed gaze edged towards him suspiciously, but Runt stilled his jaws and Kurt didn't seem to notice that his cheeks were full.

"We'd better find something tomorrow. Grunt, set up our tent in that clearing we found just outside the village. I've had enough of these hillbillies."

Runt sighed, then pushed his well-padded butt off the ground and dusted it with his hands. Signing on for this job really was a mistake. He should have stayed at home. Even his grouchy old mama's hen-pecking was better than this.

4. Not quite what we'd bargained for

Saska cautiously moved out from under the clump of bushes. The huge wasp was nowhere to be seen, but since a city boy had been in the area recently, he couldn't be too careful. He sniffed the air, making sure nobody was around. He slunk over to a raspberry bush, eating a few dripping-ripe berries and licking the juice stains from his thick fingers. A squirrel sat on a stump nearby, scolding him loudly.

Good, Saska thought. All is well again. He crept down to the creek, looking for things to eat and things he could leave for Estella. He found a snail, an almost-dead minnow, and something that looked like it might have been a mushroom before it fell in the creek. He started digging around in the creek bottom, looking for potential gifts, when a smooth stone slid into his callused palm. He rinsed the mud off of it and peered at it. It was polished, magenta pebble with some unusual markings across one side. In fact, he thought he could almost see a face sketched on it. A woman's face, young, oval, framed with a mane of dark hair. Was that Estella's face?

Yes, it definitely made him think of Estella, as if he hadn't been thinking of her already. Saska smiled, palming the rock in one thick hand. He turned to go, noticing that the squirrel he'd seen earlier had followed him to the creek. He squeaked his lips at the squirrel, which darted up a tree and scolded him. He turned to place the minnow, the snail, and the delectable mushroom on the log where he'd placed his first gifts for Estella.

As he began to walk away, the squirrel ran down the tree and snatched the mushroom off the log. Saska bellowed, shaking a fist, but the squirrel stuffed the mushroom into his mouth, climbed back up the tree and started to nibble delightedly at his stolen snack. Saska flapped a resigned hand at the squirrel and shambled back up the trail. Hopefully Estella would come this way and find his new gifts before the squirrel ate them all.

☼

Elena and I ran down the path to our favourite spot by the creek. We'd spent most of the day packing dry salted fish for the winter, layering it with bracken fronds. Our hands ached and reeked, and we couldn't wait to bathe ourselves.

As usual, Elena got there first. "C'mon, slowpoke!" she called.

I glanced down to see some more odd things placed on the same log that had displayed the old dead fish and squishy berry a few days ago. This time, the log held a little dead fish and a spiral-shelled snail. While the fish looked like it had tide recently, the snail was still very much alive, and it was munching on the fish, leaving behind a trail of slime.

I gently moved the duo onto a sliver of wood, admiring the snail's translucent brown shell, and transported them gently to the creek side. After all, the snail looked like the type that belonged in the water, and the fish must have originated there, too.

I thought about Nana's story and smiled to myself. The girl in her story had found treasures on a log, too. Maybe the odd things I'd found were sasquatch gifts, I considered. What a cute story. I wondered if Nana actually believed that sasquatches were real. She was such a good story-teller, it was hard to know what was real and what was make believe.

We stripped off our fishy shirts and soaked them in the creek, lounging in our undershirts, happy to catch the last light of autumn. Soon it would be too cold to bathe in the creek.

A masculine cough sent us scurrying from the water, peeling the wet garments back over our shoulders. Someone else must be coming to bathe; it was time to head back home.

☼

The boys crept through the bushes, Kurt in the lead, as usual. They could hear something splashing in the water, down at the creek. Runt stubbed his foot and grunted. Kurt shot him the evil eye. Runt stopped to rub his foot, then hurried to catch up with Kurt and Ferret. Runt was still burdened with the pack, but today, Ferret had a fishing net slung over his shoulder. He'd scrounged it from somewhere in the village.

Kurt scooted on his belly to peek over a rise, then he held a hand out behind him, stopping the boys abruptly. They moved to the ground and slithered up beside him, Ferret smoothly, Runt more awkwardly. Runt just wasn't made for all this sneaking, not like the other two. Five days now with no bath. He sighed. Maybe he could wash in the creek.

Lifting his head to look over the rise, Runt caught his breath. There in the creek was a rough, hairy back, and as it rose out of the water, it revealed the hairiest pair of bum-cheeks he had ever seen. The creature hummed tunelessly in a deep voice, scrubbing his armpits with creek water. He was looking away, across the creek.

Kurt gestured to Ferret and the two moved forward, net in hands. They skulked towards that broad, hairy back, then with a yell, they lunged forward, tossing the net over their prey. The hairy creature let out a huge bellow. "Got him!" Kurt whooped, triumphant.

Runt raced over and threw his arms around the hairy creature's waist. The creature thrashed about angrily, trying to swipe at his captors with his gorilla-like arms, but to no avail. He was thoroughly wrapped in the fishing net.

The boys stumbled down the path with their captive, Ferret and Kurt in the lead, Runt tripping over the fellow's hairy feet in his effort to keep his arms firmly about the creature's waist. The creature continued to bellow loudly all the way to the village.

"What's this?" Nana stopped them at the entrance to the village, a stern look on her wrinkled face.

"We caught the sasquatch!" Kurt crowed. "We got him! We'll be rich!"

"That's no sasquatch," Nana cackled. "That's my son, John. Now will you please explain just what you are doing, dragging him about dressed in nothing but a fishing net, soaking wet from head to toe?"

The boys released the hairy man and backed away, sheepish looks on their faces. John, whose well-bearded face was beet red now, extracted himself from the net and turned to face them. They scattered, Ferret and Kurt first, followed by an apologetic, bowing Runt. This was definitely not what they had in mind. John just shook his head, disbelieving.

"Where are you going?" Nana queried.

"Back to the creek, to get my clothes," John retorted, huffing. "You'd think they've never seen a naked man before!"

Nana watched him go, scratching her chin, humming thoughtfully to herself.

5. Love and hairy wishes

It had been decades since she had seen John's father, her beloved Bushy. Named after her grandfather, John was her first child, her darling love child.

Her two daughters came much later, and their father was a good man, but their relationship did not have the fierce passion of her affair with Bushy. Her daughters Maddie and Marena would in turn become mothers to Elena and Estella, the cousins who seemed close as twins, as if they had shared a womb. Nana had been around their age when she met Bushy. She hadn't been Nana yet then, or even Mama. Back then, she had still been Cora.

Young and energetic, Cora had thrived on the fresh forest air and the freedom of the new village life, blissfully unaware of her own youthful beauty. While her hopes for the future had been so limited in the city, here, the potential seemed infinite.

The villagers had cast off so many of the old ways in their effort to create a tiny utopia for themselves out here in the clean wilderness. They had left behind the terrible, face-rotting diseases, the criminal gangs, and the organ collectors who preyed upon the homeless, harvesting kidneys and corneas from their victims for resale to the rich and shameless. They had also cast off the trappings of chauvinism and prejudice; in the village, every hand was needed, and everyone's skills were welcomed. Nobody questioned where a child came from. Everyone was valued and loved.

As Cora explored her new woodland environment, Bushy had charmed her with his little gifts: a perfect spiral shell, a little pile of ripe berries, a polished stone. She came to look forward to the presents he left for her on logs and stumps, though it took him weeks to build up the courage to let her see his face.

She remembered that day fondly. She had heard a rustle in the bushes, and suspecting it was her secret admirer, she snuck around and startled him from behind. He leaped out of the bushes in a fright and ran up the trail. In his haste, he stubbed his foot and let out a huge bellow and hopped in circles, his face crinkled in pain. She ran over, caught his poor tender foot in her hands and rubbed it, crooning softly. He settled down with his behind on the ground, and she reached out hesitantly to touch his face.

He was very hairy, well-bearded and warmly coated like a bear, reddish brown in colour. His nose was broad and snubbed, and his lips were full. They quivered slightly, and she saw the fear in his eyes.

A voice called from down the trail, "Cora!" It was her father.

The bushman leaped up and was gone before she could say a word to him.

It wasn't long though before they began meeting in secret, at first just to explore one another's skin with hesitant fingers, and later to embrace hungrily. He towered head and shoulders over her, and he was powerfully muscled, but ever gentle in his touch. His confidence had grown each time they met, and with it, her delight in him had swelled until she could hardly bear to be apart from him. Nana's skin tingled with the memory of his fierce, silent embrace.

☼

John huffed and ran his fingers through his long hair to straighten it as he headed back to the creek to get his clothes. Quite a few villagers had gathered by now to see what the fuss was all about, and he could feel their eyes on his back. Had he turned, he would have seen how appreciative some of those eyes were. He was completely unaware of the effect his large, muscular body had on the eyes of the other adults in the village.

John had always been a bit of a loner. When he was younger, the other youths would share their dreams of running off to the city to find... something. It was never really clear to him exactly what they hoped to find there.

A few young folks did run off to the city, but they always returned within a few months, humbled, saying very little about what they had been through. They threw their backs into their work and never complained about the village life again. John's oldest sister, Maddie, could be found down at the creek every day for months after she got back from the city, scrubbing and scrubbing at her skin, though she looked perfectly clean to his young eyes. She never did say what she was trying to wash away.

John had never longed for the city. It was the wilderness that called to him. Sometimes, even Halftree Village felt crowded, and then he'd pack up a scant few things and wander out to live in the bush for weeks or even months at a time. His ma would tell the others that he'd gone on a walkabout. Really, he'd just gone off so he could think clearly.

When he was away from other people, he could truly hear the forest around him. He felt as if he could understand the calls of the animals, and could even hear the slow thoughts of the plants as they extended their roots into the soil and their tendrils to the sky.

When he returned home from one of his walkabouts, he brought back rare plants and mushrooms which could be used as medicine. People would come to him with their rashes, wounds and digestive ailments; he was respected as a medicine-man in the village.

Fresh from the woods, he felt calm, rejuvenated, and his eyes and skin were clear. He beamed at everyone, and they reflected his contentment with smiles of their own. He could hold onto that feeling of peace for a few weeks, but sooner or later, he knew he'd have to head out again.

Come to think of it, he hadn't gone on a walkabout in quite some time. He was due for a recharge.

☼

Saska stretched each of his grimy toes, sighing and thinking about his family. He desperately wished that he wasn't so lonely anymore. His loneliness sat like a stubborn ache in his chest, threatening to push tears into his eyes.

A little squirrel edged towards him. It looked like the same one that had been hanging around earlier. He frowned and waved it away, but it leaped up onto his head and nestled itself into his woolly mat of hair. He darted out of his cavern, thinking that he might startle the squirrel enough to make it run off. The cheeky rodent stirred a little, but it hung on tight. Resigned, Saska decided to go look for something to eat, whether or not he had a squirrel nesting in his fur.

Just as he headed uphill towards the mountains, the squirrel sprang off of his head and into the branches of a tree, scolding sharply. Flocks of birds took to the sky, circling, their wings flashing in the sunlight. Alarmed, Saska ducked into some bushes, then peeped out through a gap in the foliage. A fuzzy, brown bear the size of a fox wandered by, sniffing the ground. Saska knew that its mother was probably around, so he stayed still.

Moments later, an enormous cave bear stormed into view, nudging the baby along with her snout. She paid Saska no attention. He waited until she had moved out of sight with her little one, then he waited some more, long enough for the squirrel to settle down and climb back into his fur, and long enough for the birds to settle back into the trees and resume their chatter.

Higher up in the hills, Saska found a hawk feather and a few milky-red cranberries. These would make lovely gifts for Estella. He popped one of the cranberries into his mouth. Hmmm...Saska thought. Not nearly ripe enough, but it'll have to do. He ate several more, then picked some to take back with him for Estella. As he foraged, the squirrel wandered off on some task of its own.

Looking around, he wondered where the squirrel had gone. He scratched his neck, finding pine nuts buried in the thick woolly fuzz of his neck hair. So that's what the little creature had been up to back there! He smiled and added a few of the nuts to Estella's gift.

The sun's light seemed to shudder as a dark fist of cloud swelled in its path. With a low rumble of thunder, the rain began, lightly at first. By the time Saska made it back to his cave, the sky was dark and threatening, and the paths were being torn into mud by thick, heavy drops of rain.

6. When it rains

Runt sat with the village boys, his feet bare. The soles of his feet were tender, but he'd ditched his city boots anyway. If these boys could run around barefoot, why couldn't he? His mother wasn't here to tell him not to, anyway.

He loved tagging along with these guys. Sometimes one of them would offer him a bit of help or advice about something he wasn't familiar with. How to gut a fish, for starters. In the city, fish were pale slabs wrapped in plastic. You bought them at all-sales, or if you didn't have the money, you might find some in the dumpster out back.

He was suspicious at first, narrowing his eyes at the boys and trying to figure out if they were just leading him on. They seemed genuine. Nobody had laughed at him yet. This was nothing like the city, where even your friends were out to get you. Everyone climbed over top of everyone else, trying to get a better view of things.

Ferret hung around outside the group of boys, his eyes shifting one way, then the next. He didn't join in, but he didn't leave, either. He eyed Runt thoughtfully, scratching his skinny back with soiled fingernails. Runt could feel those eyes prickling on his skin, making him feel self-conscious.

At a holler from Kurt, Ferret and Runt both jumped. What did he want now?

Kurt stormed over, scoffing. "What do you think you're doing? Grunt, what's with the feet? You're not going local on us, are you?"

"The name's not Grunt. It's Runt," Runt mumbled.

"Yeah right. Let's go, Grunt. If we don't rustle a sasquatch soon, the boss is going to come looking for us." Kurt looked worried.

Ferret and Runt followed Kurt back to their campsite, Ferret slinking along in his usual manner, and Runt hobbling, his tender feet unused to the pounding they were getting from the sand and rocks. At the tent, he wiggled his feet back into his sweaty boots, the sand and grit sticking to the sides. It was still hot as summer, though the first of the leaves were turning golden. The sticky dirt between his toes felt awful.

"What are we going to do now?" he whined.

"Let's go trap ourselves a sasquatch," Kurt replied, confidently. He was tapping something into his eWare. Runt peered over his shoulder.

GoldenBoy23 / Caught a hairy man #ohcrud/

Ferret just scratched himself some more, then wiped his nose on a grubby sleeve. He didn't look too convinced.

"Well? What are you waiting for?" Kurt bellowed, shouldering Runt aside. "Grab the gear and let's go."

Sighing, Runt picked up the dusty backpack full of sasquatch-huntin' gear and followed Kurt and Ferret into the woods.

That was when they heard the first rumble of thunder.

☼

It poured for the next three days. Lightning tore brilliant rents through the black cloud, and thunder shook the trees. Runt spent much of his time hunkered down in the tent with Kurt and Ferret, feeling totally miserable. The space was too small, the tent was leaky, and Kurt kept sending him off on random errands.

On the third evening, his back soaked to the skin, Runt was out digging around hopelessly for dry twigs to start a fire. By now his nose was dripping like Ferret's, and the skin around it was raw. He'd never felt so unhappy. Ferret had slunk off somewhere, and Kurt was getting so cranky Runt was actually relieved to be out of the tent, despite the rain.

He envied the villagers in their dry cabins. He even envied Ferret, wherever he was, for not being here right now.

"What's taking so long?" Kurt yelled. "Get that fire going, Grunt. I don't know about you, but I want my dinner."

If he calls me Grunt one more time, Runt thought....

"Grunt! You deaf or what?"

Well, that's it, Runt thought. *Paycheque or not*, I QUIT.

He threw down his meagre handful of kindling and stomped off towards the village.

"Where do you think you're going?" rang Kurt's angry voice, more faintly. Runt kept walking through the heavy drizzle towards the warm glow of the village.

The sound of voices and the smell of wood smoke told Runt that the villagers weren't huddled in their cabins after all. They had strung up several tarps at the centre of the village, forming a rough circle around a large, cozy bonfire. They were gathered in small groups under the tarps. One group sang together, their voices a comfortable low chant, accompanied by a hollow drum rhythm. One of the girls was sitting on a hollowed-out log which she beat with her hands in a complex pattern.

Others seemed rapt in intimate conversation. Still others worked around a large cauldron, filling it with root vegetables, herbs and fish. Together, two burly men lifted the cauldron and dropped it close to the fire.

Runt spotted Ethan sitting with his arm around a pretty, dark-eyed girl. He sidled in to sit down alongside them. Ethan grinned and handed him a chunk of raw wood and a whittling knife. Runt grinned back.

"Hey, have you seen Ferret?" Runt asked. Ethan gestured towards a tarp on the other side of the fire. There was Ferret, the little rodent, warm and dry, a smug look on his pinched face. He held a steaming mug in his hands. Runt scowled at him, then turned to his whittling. *I'll carve a little weasel,* he thought. That would make him feel better. It was just like Ferret to slink off like that, leaving him with the chores.

Ferret worked his way round the fire, staying under the tarps. Runt didn't notice him until Ferret cleared his throat right in his ear. He jumped and snapped, "Don't do that!"

"You bailing on this job?"

Runt looked at Ferret suspiciously. What if Ferret tried to make him go back? Would he and Kurt drag Runt off and force him to continue this useless search? But Ferret just looked back at him innocently, wide-eyed.

Runt nodded. "I've had it," he said.

"Well," Ferret said with a sly grin, "more rewards for me, I guess." He sauntered off, avoiding the open, dripping gaps between the tarps, and disappeared behind the fire.

Playing both sides, I see, thought Runt. *Typical.*

As the rain poured down outside, Nana could hear friendly chatter and snatches of song drifting into her cabin. In her hands, the wooden shuttle slid back and forth, back and forth across her loom. Her lanterns glowed, and the air was pungent with the smell of drying herbs which hung from her rafters all around.

As her shuttle flew, Nana hummed to herself. And if someone happened to peek in the window, squinting to see through the rain-slick glass, the pattern on the loom might seem to dance with shapes and figures. Every now and then, if they looked closely, they might see a flash like sunshine dart by, quickly buried in the pattern. After all, there were things to be hidden here, and someone had to do the hiding.

The occasional bounty hunter this village could handle, through gentle misdirection and subterfuge. But there was something here that outsiders must never, ever suspect, lest their way of life be ruined forever. Deep within its heart, this land was rich with gold.

7. Things to be hidden

I strolled down towards the creek, loving the clean, fresh smell in the air. Three days of rain had polished the earth until it gleamed brightly. The leaves shone, and birds sang in the woods all around me.

When I got to my favourite spot, I dug my toes into the silt of the bank. The rains had swollen the creek; where it had been up to my calves a few days ago, it was now thigh-deep. The water burbled along enthusiastically. Here and there near the shore, a tiny fish struggled against the current. Reeds that had stood on the bank were now swept down into the water, and there they swung like wet hair, their roots firm.

I heard a light scuffing sound and turned. Uncle John approached with a day pack on his back and a water bottle in his hand. He wore sandals and light travelling clothes. He smiled at me, then knelt at the creek to fill his water bottle.

"Going on a walkabout, then?" I asked.

He nodded his assent.

"Think you will find some more Usnea? Nana said she's just about out, but I haven't been able to find any around here. We'll need it for the winter."

"You're just like Nana," he teased, ruffling my hair. "You'll have the rest of us co-ordinated in no time."

I ducked my head shyly, smiling. It was certainly no insult to be compared to Nana. At times, it seemed like she held she village together in her quiet, stern way. She never really ordered anyone about, but everyone usually did what she wanted anyway.

John turned up the path and headed out. "Be safe," I called. He waved, barely turning. His mind was already ahead of him, out there in the wilderness.

I stripped off my shirt, hiked up my skirt and tucked it into the waistband. Though the water was icy, it felt good to wash after three days of confinement. The smell of smoke from the campfire sloughed from my skin.

I picked up a stone, a translucent, ice-white agate. Rubbing the silt from it, I decided it was special enough to keep. I tucked it into my waistband.

A faint sound from across the creek startled me and I turned, heart suddenly pounding. At first, I saw nothing there but the usual bushes, trees and stumps, the reeds and grasses along the creek side still slick with rainwater. Was it just a bird, or some other wild animal rustling the bushes?

A dark, hairy shape moved, barely visible through the leaves. Possibly a bear, rummaging around in search of grub? There were quite a few of them around at this time of year, filling their bellies in preparation for winter. We had to keep an eye out when we were picking berries, so we didn't bump into one by mistake.

My breath caught as a hairy, human-like hand reached out of the bushes towards a stump.

The hand opened, and slowly, a little stream of cranberries rolled out onto the stump.

The hand withdrew.

I pretended to keep washing, but I watched intently out of the corner of my eye. A few heartbeats later, the hand returned. This time, it held the striped and speckled brown feather of a hawk. It gently placed the feather down beside the berries, then disappeared back into the bushes.

Thinking of Nana's stories, I wondered whether someone was playing a trick on me, or if I was dreaming. I called softly, "Uncle?" There was no reply. My heart was still beating quickly; I could hear the blood rushing in my ears.

Deliberately, I got dressed, then I followed an indirect route over to the stump. Sure enough, there was a little pile of berries, with a few pine nuts mixed in. And there was the feather. I pinched a berry between my fingers. It felt real enough. It was a high-bush cranberry; they didn't grow in the immediate area, but I knew where they could be found, higher up in the hills. I popped it into my mouth. Delicious!

Tucking the feather into my hair, I turned to examine the bushes. They were empty. However, the rain had left the ground soft, and I could see a large, bare footprint where the creature must have been standing. It definitely wasn't Uncle John playing a trick on me. His feet hadn't been bare, and they weren't nearly this large.

I should be afraid, I thought. But for some reason, I wasn't. Maybe Nana's stories had numbed me to all caution, but this creature didn't frighten me at all, even if it had been watching me bathe.

I scooped up the rest of the berries and turned to go. Then, impulsively, I plucked the white agate out of my waistband, kissed it lightly, and placed it on the stump.

☼

Saska watched Estella walk away from the creek. After she disappeared from sight, he held his breath for a few heartbeats, and then he cautiously made his way back over to the stump. He picked up the stone she'd placed there and sniffed it. He could smell her touch on it still. His full lips curled upwards, revealing a row of strong, white teeth. He curled his palm around the stone, happily.

Saska took the long way around to his cave, picking the occasional hazelnut or berry as he walked. At one point, his squirrel friend began following him from the safety of the trees, chattering to himself. Saska shelled a hazelnut with his teeth and set it on a log. He backed away and watched as the little squirrel edged down the tree, bit by bit, warily. The squirrel finally made it to the log, where he looked at Saska and chirped loudly before snatching the nut and darting back up the tree. Saska chuckled.

He headed up the rise that led to his cave. Suddenly, the squirrel scolded loudly from above. Alerted, Saska dropped down into some bushes. Voices came to him faintly then, followed by a whiff of city-boy stink on the breeze. He could only detect two of them this time. The big one wasn't with them.

Silently, he slunk away, higher into the hills, leaving his cave behind for now. It was too small, anyway, he decided. It was time to look for a larger home for the winter.

☼

Kurt was sure they were looking in the right area. There were caves in these hills, and caves meant beasties. He just hoped they found a sasquatch, not a bear. He had no desire to tangle with a bear. Besides, since the unfortunate loss of their tranquilizer wasp, they had no way to stun a large beast. They were counting on being able to over-power the beast and tie it up, though without Runt's help, it wouldn't be easy.

Kurt was the brains of the crew, not the muscles. And Ferret was... well, he was Ferret. He was small, but he was strong. You never knew for sure if you could count on him. Sometimes he surprised Kurt with his ingenuity, and other times, he was nowhere to be seen.

Earlier today he'd tapped a quick and deliberately vague micro.

GoldenBoy23 /Yes #ontherighttrack/

He checked his eWare and a couple of guys had hit him back.

Trololol666 @GoldenBoy23 /WTF man?/

DollyPollyAnna @ Trololol666 GoldenBoy23 / musta found some joy juice, hahaha/

He shook his head and smiled, but didn't bother to elaborate. It was fun dragging these guys along for the ride, in a virtual sense.

The tranquilizer wasp trap had been an epic failure. After it was tripped once, they managed to recapture the wasp, only to have the box tipped over by Runt's clumsy clod-hoppers, letting the huge insect loose inside their tent. All they could do was holler and open the tent flaps. Of course the wasp didn't leave right away. It clung to the side of the tent, the three boys cowering as far away from it as possible.

"Catch it!" Kurt had ordered Runt and Ferret, but the two just looked at him like he had three heads. Slowly, the wasp had ambled over to the door of the tent and flew off. Quite honestly, Kurt hoped he'd never see the thing again. He hated wasps.

But now he was left to think of another way to trap the beast, and with one less pair of hands to do it. What could he do? Dig a pit and lay branches over it, then pounce on the thing when it fell in? That might work.

He signalled to Ferret, and the two headed back to the village to borrow some shovels, ropes and fishing nets.

☼

Back at the village, I joined Nana on her porch. She was perched on a straight-backed wooden chair, a basket of fishing nets beside her. She ran each net through her hands, checking for damage.

I rocked back on my heels, taking a handful of nets to help Nana with her inspection. We set aside any that were torn, and later, we'd repair them with heavy nettle twine.

"Nana," I asked, "Can you tell me more about the sasquatch from your stories? Did he leave you any other gifts?"

Nana smiled fondly. "How do you know the sasquatch is real, girl?"

I rolled my eyes. "Nana, I've seen one."

"What?" she started, rising suddenly from her chair. The nets fell forgotten around her ankles.

"Really, I'm sure it was a sasquatch. He gave me this feather." I pulled the feather out of my hair and placed it in her outstretched hand. She turned it over and over between her fingers, her brow furrowed deeply.

"Child, this is very serious. It's not safe for him around here. Not with these city boys snooping around."

I raised an eyebrow at her. "Do you really think they could catch him?"

"They caught your Uncle John," she snorted.

"Uncle's gone on a walkabout now," I remembered. "I wonder if I should have asked him to stay. If anyone can handle those city boys, it's him."

Nana tapped her foot impatiently, pursing her lips. "Have you spoken with him yet?"

"Yes, I talked to him just as he was leaving the village."

"Not John, child, the sasquatch. Have you made any contact?"

"No," I said, confused. "I didn't know they could speak. I just caught sight of him for the first time today."

"Where?"

"Down at the creek, at that spot where the best agates are found."

"Take me there," Nana ordered. Puzzled, I took her arm and led the way.

At the creek, Nana poked around, sniffing stones and tapping the bushes. I showed her where I had found the footprint. I was about to mention the agate I'd left behind for my hairy friend, but thought better of it. Nana seemed pretty upset already, and I didn't want to make things worse.

I still wasn't sure what she was so worried about. Was this really just about the city boys? Or did she think the sasquatch would harm me? Somehow, I knew that would never happen.

"We need to warn him away," Nana decided. "It's not safe for him around the village right now."

"He is really very shy, and he seems to be very good at hiding. What is the worst thing that could happen?"

"Take me back home and I'll tell you the rest of my story. Let me tell you what happened to my sasquatch friend," said Nana.

☼

"Bushy was my first love," Nana said, settling back in her chair. I settled down beside her, mermaid style, to listen. "It all began with his little gifts. It was early summer when I began finding treasures piled on logs and stumps in the woods. He left me berries, sometimes a special rock or feather, and once he left me a stone with a perfect fossilized shell embedded in it. I still have that stone here on my windowsill." She sighed.

"We became close friends, then sweethearts, that summer. But it wasn't long before the bounty hunters came from the city. To this day, I think someone must have tipped them off. But I never found out who."

Nana's eyes grew distant. I wrapped my arms tightly around my legs, anxiously. Then I closed my eyes and felt myself travelling into her story.

"Bushy and I were snuggled in his cave. The birdsong of summer filled the air. I ran my fingers through his hair, teasing out the tangles and burrs. A low rumble came from his throat, like a purr. Our contentment was delicious. Then we heard unfamiliar male voices, shattering the peaceful sounds of the forest. All the birds fell silent.

The strange men passed by the mouth of the cave. We were fortunate.

Once they were gone from sight, I kissed Bushy quickly, then made my way back to the village to find out what was going on. Everyone was astir. Apparently, a team of bounty hunters had been through here earlier, promising rewards and threatening violence, cajoling and forcing the villagers to help them locate unusual wildlife. They were especially interested in any large, hairy bushmen that might be hanging around the area.

Worried, I ran back to Bushy's cave. He was gone.

Frantic, I began searching the area, circling more and more widely out from his cave. I couldn't find any clues.

I returned home just as the sun was setting. That night, I could barely choke down my meal. My mother looked worried, but nobody questioned me.

Early the next morning, as soon as it was light enough to see, I ran back through the woods up to Bushy's cave. It was normally quite a long walk, but that morning, I made it there in the time it took for the sun to rise a thumb's width in the sky. There was no sign of Bushy.

Not far from Bushy's cave, I found a clearing where the bounty hunters had set up camp. They had rigged up a rope net, and inside that net, there was my dearest Bushy! Alarmed, I started to run forward, then I saw the city men digging through their supplies on the other side of their tent. I ducked behind some bushes and settled down to wait. There was no way I was going to let them get away with this.

My poor, dear Bushy sat, hunkered down, his hands bound behind him, the net wrapped around him. The entire bundle was lashed to a tree. What could I do? I didn't even have a knife on me.

Thinking quickly, I made my way back to Bushy's cave. There, I collected several shards of stone that Bushy used as blades. I hoped they would be sharp enough to cut his bindings.

I snuck back to the city men's camp, trying to think of a plan. Oh, how I wished I had someone with me to help! Anyone, a friend, a brother, even my mother. But there was just me.

Knowing I couldn't overpower the men, I decided to try and trick them. I spotted a moderately sized boulder on a nearby hillside. Sneaking over, I got behind it and began working it loose. I wiggled it back and forth, and soon it broke free and began to rumble down the hillside. By the time it got near the camp, it was crashing through the bush.

"Bear!" I shouted. "Look out for the bear!"

Alarmed, the city men leaped up, looking around. In a panic, one of them climbed a tree. The other two ran off into the bush.

This was my chance. I snuck in behind Bushy and sawed frantically at his bonds. Looking encouraged now, he began tugging on them, trying to work his hands free. I saw how chafed his poor, dear skin was where the ropes had dug into his wrists.

"Hey, what do you think you're doing?" the man hollered at me from up the tree.

Sobbing, I kept working at Bushy's bonds. Just as the other two men came back into the clearing to investigate, the rope broke free!

Bushy tore the net off and roared, pounding his powerful chest like a gorilla. He rose up to his full height, half again as tall as a typical human. It was a side of Bushy that I had never seen before! It was almost enough to terrify me, and I could see the men shrink back, turning pale.

The men backed away. The one in the tree edged his way up further out of reach, whimpering.

Bushy ran one way, and I ran the other.

I wish I could tell you that this story has a happy ending, but it doesn't. The bounty hunters chased Bushy up into the mountains, but eventually, they lost his trail. They passed through the village again three days later, empty handed, looking unhappy and worn out.

I never saw my poor, dear Bushy again.

I hope to this day that he still lives out there, somewhere in the wilderness, and that he is happy and contented. I hope that he remembers my love for him. I have very fond memories of the time we had together.

So that, my dear child, is the story of my sasquatch love. And that is why your hairy friend is in great danger right now."

"What can we do?" I asked. "I won't let them hurt him!"

"Here is what I want you to do," Nana said, and she bent towards my ear to whisper. Nodding, lump in my throat, I took in every word.

8. The road least travelled

Dr. Ronald Wigglesworth paused to study the view behind him. He was in the rear of a small group, comprised of a bounty hunter and two of his own dedicated research assistants. They followed a deer track that led to the village nearest the spot where they'd been dropped off by the chopper.

He straightened his white Tilley hat, pulled his knee socks up, and began walking again. He presented quite a striking image, he knew, with his canvas shorts, hiking sandals and pressed shirt. A sturdy walking stick was the finishing touch on the outfit. The whiskers of his white beard marked his wisdom, and he knew they were essential to his status as an expert anthropologist with a mature career. He'd have to get one of his assistants to take his photo out here, in situ, for the jacket cover of his next book.

Dr. Wigglesworth was a specialist in early-hominid life-forms, and he had been called to speak on the subject at numerous international conferences. He was the author of several authoritative texts on the subject of modern-day non-human hominids: Bigfoot, Sasquatch and Yeti.

Unfortunately, the creatures were very shy and rare. His studies so far had been based solely on anecdotes and the occasional trace of DNA found in a tuft of hair or a piece of bone. And why could nobody get a clear photograph of one? All the pictures looked as if Vaseline had been smeared over the lens of the camera. He sighed majestically.

With this trip, he believed his luck was about to change. Some kind of energy field threw off geo-location devices in this area, so they had to resort to old-fashioned maps and compasses. It took him back to his old grad student days; at least he was adept at using conventional tools.

He had scoured the records, and a collection of old diaries and maps had led him precisely to this quadrant. There was solid evidence of a sasquatch in this area. While the diaries dated back forty years or more, the life expectancy of a sasquatch was unknown. Besides, he figured where there had been one sasquatch, there would likely be others.

The bounty hunter had sent three men ahead, and he was confident that they would have gathered information from the locals, if they hadn't actually trapped a sasquatch already. It would be worth the enormous expense of this expedition just to get the hairy beast into his lab. He would be the first to study a real, live sasquatch! He would surely receive a commendation from the University for this, as well as numerous international awards.

"Doc," the bounty hunter called back to him. He was a crude man who just went by the moniker 'Boss.' He was a stocky man with a rough face and few words.

"Yes?" Ronald replied. Though it was a small thing, he just couldn't bring himself to call the man Boss.

Boss waved him over. Drawing up beside him, next to a huge, old tree which had been split by lightning decades ago, he saw Halftree Village sprawled in the valley below. Tendrils of smoke rose from the chimney of a few of the weathered wooden huts, built in the classic turn-of-century style that was typical of these back-to-the-land settlements. Most huts had a covered front porch, and the construction materials were hand-worked and solid, though grey now with age. Packed dirt paths wove between the huts, with just a few kitchen gardens scratched into the earth here and there. There was a central clearing, marred by the blackened smears of three stone-ringed fire-pits. Very few of the villagers were visible.

It was time for him to take the lead. He'd soon ingratiate himself with these natives, collect his sasquatch, and head back to the drop-off point in time for the next pick-up. The pilot had been instructed to fly by every three days to check for them.

Boss reached the top of the rise and saw a collection of little shacks, all clustered together in the next valley. A few grubby villagers were hanging about. He waved over to Doc Moneybags and watched the little, knobby-kneed man huff his way up the hill. It was amazing the old coot had made it this far. He sure was out of shape.

Doc's eyes lit up when he saw Halftree village, like this place was some kind of treasure. Boss just shook his head and let the guy charge down the hill, his bespeckled assistants fumbling with their gear and racing to catch up with him. He ambled along behind, taking his time. It wasn't like they were going to miss the train or anything. What did time matter in a little village like this?

He really didn't understand why Doc had insisted on coming along. The crew could have brought the sasquatch back into the city. In fact, it would have been easier without these academics tagging along. But Doc kept saying he needed to see the sasquatch "insecure," or some such nonsense.

As he approached the village, he cast his eyes about for his crew. He spotted their tent in a clearing just north of the village. They'd strung up a line and it was decorated with socks, underwear and other random, colourful bits of clothing. A small circle of stones outlined a crude fire-pit, but the fire was out. The site appeared to be deserted at the moment. *Good,* he thought. *Can't have them lazing about all day.*

☼

Ferret had dust all over him from a day of hard digging. He and Kurt had been working on their sasquatch trap. It was a large pit, lined with a fishing net. A rope ran around the edges of the net, so it could be cinched tight. Their plan was to return to the pit tomorrow and lay spruce boughs across the top. Then they would take turns hiding in the bushes, holding the end of the rope, ready to snare the sasquatch.

Something was niggling at him though, a vague worry. Why would the sasquatch step on the trap? Didn't they need some kind of bait? But what kind of bait would work on a sasquatch?

Kurt stopped abruptly just before they arrived at the village. Ferret almost ran into him. "Oh crud," Kurt muttered under his breath. There, right ahead of them, poking around their campsite, was the hard, mean profile of the Boss.

☼

I ran down the trail towards the fish camp, looking for Elena. I ran into some of the village boys first; they were on their way back to the village. I skirted around them, waving away their grins and cheerful banter. There was Elena, tagging along behind with Ethan.

"I need your help," I gasped, trying to slow my breathing down.

"What is it?" Elena looked worried.

"I can't tell you here. Just come."

Ethan squeezed her hand and waved to her as we ran back up the trail.

She blew him a kiss.

"There's trouble," I said after we'd passed the cluster of boys again. "We need to pack up a few things and go into the bush. Grab some snacks, water, and rope. I'll meet you at the creek trail."

We split up, and I hastily filled a stuff sack with survival gear. I wasn't sure how long our task would take, so I brought enough food to last four or five days.

A short time later, Elena met me by the creek. She wore sandals, and she carried a stuffed backpack. It was a good thing we were both used to these sorts of adventures!

"So, why so mysterious? What is this all about, anyway?"

I took a minute to think about how to explain it. Slowly, I began.

"Remember Nana's story about the sasquatch?" She nodded. "Well, remember those weird things we found on that log over there?" I pointed to the log where we'd found the strange little gifts.

"Yes, what about it? You don't really think…." Elena looked sceptical.

I nodded. "Yes, for real. I saw him this morning, right over there." I pointed to the bushes where the sasquatch had been hiding earlier.

Elena stomped over sceptically and poked around in the bushes. Her eyes grew wide. "Holy moly, check out the size of this footprint!"

"I know. Nana says he's in danger, and we have to help him. I won't let those bounty hunters find him!"

Elena nodded resolutely. "What do we need to do? Whatever it is, let's do it."

"Nana told me what to do. Let's go."

I led the way, up into the hills.

We hiked until the sun was low in the sky. When we came to a clearing, I held out my hand to stop Elena. Together, we studied the clearing. Someone had been digging here. They'd dug a huge hole, large enough for a man to disappear into. A pile of soil and a stack of fishing nets sat beside the pit. Nobody seemed to be around.

"Nana said we'd find something like this here. Now it's our turn to lay a trap."

Walking back into the bushes, Elena and I started to fill our hands with berries. When my berry-holding hand was full, I transferred the berries to the front of my shirt, which I held out to make a sort of pocket. Elena followed suit.

Once we had several large handfuls of berries each, we dropped them into the pit. "These will be the perfect bait… for a bear," I chuckled. While the pit would be deep enough to trap a man, there was no way it would keep a bear from escaping. If anyone could chase away those city boys, it was an angry bear. We wiped away our footprints with a spruce bough and headed farther up into the hills.

We spotted a cave just as night was falling. It had been carved into the sandy hillside, and though its entrance was low enough that we had to stoop to enter, we found it to be quite roomy within. Though it appeared to have been inhabited at one time, no beasts were at home. We set up camp on the smooth dirt floor of the cavern and settled down for the night.

"What did Nana say to do next?"

"Next," I answered mysteriously, "she said we need to collect someone in the morning. Someone who is in grave danger right now. Then we will go find Uncle John."

We snuggled together under our single blanket and let the sounds of the night lull us to sleep. We would need to make an early start come morning.

9. New friends and old commitments

The sound of a squirrel's chatter woke me just before dawn. Sitting up, stretching, I watched the little guy dance at the entrance to the cave, his call a stutter punctuating his little hops. He seemed to be quite upset about something.

Then I saw a large, hairy head peek around the mouth of the cave. For a split second, I thought it was a bear, and my heart leaped into my throat. I reached back to shake Elena's leg.

I thought the little squirrel was in serious trouble as it raced straight towards the hairy mop. But to my amazement, the squirrel hopped up onto the hairy head and continued its rant from that perch. That was when I realized that the brown fur didn't belong to a bear. It was my sasquatch friend.

Slowly, making no sudden movements, I crawled forward. Elena sat up, rubbing her eyes and mumbling. Then she froze. "Estella?" she croaked.

"It's okay," I said softly. I wasn't sure if I was talking to Elena, to myself, or to my hairy friend. Perhaps to all three of us. Not to mention the squirrel.

"We need to leave this place," I explained. I felt like somehow it would all be okay if I just kept talking. "It's not safe for you. There are bounty hunters in the area."

The woolly head cocked sideways, as if listening. Then a grin spread across the big, hairy face. The squirrel had handfuls of my friend's hair in each of its little fists. It was still chattering angrily. They were such a sight I couldn't help laughing nervously. Then Elena started to laugh, too. The sasquatch barked, and we both jumped, but then we saw that his shoulders were shaking with laughter. Soon the three of us were rolling on the ground, we were laughing so hard. The squirrel finally gave up on his rant and hopped over to a rock, where he proceeded to dig, sending bits of dirt and fluff flying, stuffing seeds into his face. Apparently he had stowed his food stash in this cave.

Our laughter stilled, settling into the occasional chuckle. Then we heard voices in the distance, coming from down the hill. It was time to go.

The three of us set off stealthily over the hill, the sasquatch towering head and shoulders over me and Elena. He seemed quite unafraid of us, and he reached out to brush my arm from time to time. The little squirrel tagged along, hopping from tree to tree.

Yes, it was definitely time to go find Uncle John. I sighed, happily. How I loved adventures!

Runt followed the village boys as they left the fish camp. He was tired, his hands were raw, he smelled of fish, and his face was sunburned. The skin was peeling off his forehead in strips. Nonetheless, he was happier than he could remember being in a very long time.

One of the old folks had shown him how to tie a fish lure, and that was his latest obsession. He figured he was quite good at it, much better than he was at whittling. His left hand still bore cuts from where the whittling knife had slipped off the wood and into his flesh.

Fish lures, now that he could do. He kept an eye out for feathers, tufts of fluff, and hollow sticks to use in his lures. The best one he'd made so far had a nice tuft of brown wool that he'd found in the tent. It had an excellent loft to it, and he loved the way the wool danced when it hit the water.

It amazed him at first to see how these people could survive just on what they caught, or picked, or found in the woods. He was accustomed to opening a packet whenever he was hungry. Back home, he would have been snacking on Cheezy Strings or eating Tikka Hearty Meal directly from the box. Here, he just had to look around and there were berries, hazelnuts, and other edible things all around him. He felt like his eyes were opening for the first time as he learned what was safe to eat, and what wasn't.

Stomach rumbling, he made it back to the village just in time to witness the arrival of the Boss.

Crud.

Head down, he shuffled into the village behind the other boys, hoping he wouldn't be noticed. How he wished he'd never signed on with that crew.

☼

GoldenBoy23 /the heat is on #ohcruditstheboss/

Kurt and Ferret went reluctantly down to the camp to meet the Boss.

"Well?" the rough-faced man snapped at them. "Don't you two look a mess. Anything to report?"

Kurt and Ferret glanced at one another sheepishly. Kurt made a quick attempt at brushing the dust off his once-dapper clothes, pressing his button shirt flat with his hands. "Yes sir, absolutely sir. We found a number of clues, and we are just hours from securing the sasquatch."

Boss pursed his lips sceptically and scratched his scalp, his thinning hair dancing like greasy spiders. Ferret suppressed a nervous giggle.

"What evidence do you have?"

"We found signs of habitation in a cave-riddled region not far from here. Also we almost had a sighting, and we found a tuft of hair. Here, I have it in my pocket." Kurt began digging about in his shirt pocket.

"What do you mean, you ALMOST had a sighting?"

"Well, we saw the bushes move..." Kurt was still digging in his pocket, a bit more frantically now. He had pulled out an electronic device, a few bits of string and a book of matches, but there was no sign of the tuft of hair. He distinctly remembered putting it into a plastic bag, but there was no sign of the bag, either. Maybe it was in the tent.

"You saw the BUSHES move? And how do you know there was a sasquatch in the bushes? How do you know it wasn't a person, or a goose, or a fudge-riddled bear?"

"We found the tuft of hair...."

"WHAT tuft of hair? The one that doesn't exist?" Boss was getting red in the face now. Ferret thought this might be a good moment to make himself scarce. He started to slink away, but Boss barked at him, "Where do YOU think you're going? Get back here. And where's Runt?"

Ferret snapped to attention. He and Kurt looked at one another guiltily, avoiding eye contact with the Boss. It was astonishing how that man could make a guy feel guilty, even when he had nothing to feel guilty about.

"I haven't seen Runt lately. He went local on us," Kurt whined.

"Well, go get him. I'm not cutting anyone loose until I've got some profit out of this madcap expedition," Boss snapped.

Kurt elbowed Ferret and gave him a stern look. Glad for the excuse to get away, Ferret scooted off to look for Runt.

☼

Nana slid the shuttle back and forth across her weaving, the light of her lantern casting long shadows across the room. This part of the pattern was mostly blue and green, but here and there, a flicker of brown or silver darted in like a beast or fish, quickly buried within the earthy tones of the fabric.

The cloth she wove would soon become a piece of clothing or a blanket. Into that cloth she wove charms and stories, things to expose, and things to keep hidden. The magic of her weaving was part of everyday life around here. It was made to be worn.

As Nana wove, she thought back to her conversation with Estella. She had given the girl some vague instructions, yet she felt confident that Estella would know what to do. If anyone had inherited her talents, guile and spirit, it was Estella. She had chosen the girl as her heir, the one who she'd pass her knowledge and skills along to, knowing that someone would have to take over from her someday. Estella had shown some skill with the loom, and she was quick to understand the way of things.

The girl would do her part, out there in the woods, keeping certain secrets safe. And Nana would do her own part, here at the loom, and with a carefully placed word here and there amongst the villagers and their occasional guests. A certain twist of the weave, or a careful omission in one's choice of words, and all would be well again in the village.

☼

John hiked deep into the hills. By day's end, he came to a familiar spot where he had often camped before. He dropped his pack then walked over to a small creek to refill his water bottle. The water ran clear and burbling here, free of any silt or urban contamination. He drank deeply. The water tasted of fresh ice melt from high in the mountains.

A sitting stump and a ring of stones marked the site of his old fire pit. He cleared out a bit of rubble that had collected there, then he began combing the nearby bushes for dry sticks to use as kindling. Bending down over some brush, he felt eyes on his back. Sensing no threat, he continued collecting sticks, then he stood upright and turned slowly. Someone was seated on the stump.

It was a large, hairy man who would have towered even over John, who was not a small man himself. The man wore no clothing; instead, he was garbed in a thick, brown pelt. His wrinkled face was ringed with grizzled fur. His forehead was high and domed, and it jutted out slightly at the brow. His brown eyes, large and flat as pebbles, twinkled.

"Little John."

A huge smile cracked across John's broad face. "Bushy! Papa! I haven't seen you in years." Dropping his armload of kindling beside the fire pit, he stepped forward and stooped down to embrace the hairy man. In his arms, he felt once again as if he'd come home.

10. The simple matter of evidence

The next morning, the crew was finally reassembled and ready to go set the trap they'd built up in the hills. For some reason, the old fella who Boss called Doc insisted on coming, along with his two hapless assistants. The assistants carried a large metal box between them. Doc called it his 'quipment. He said he needed to gather 'live' evidence of the sasquatch, and whatever was in the box would help him do just that.

It was a much more arduous trek to the site now that they had all these other people in tow. Kurt led the way, followed by Ferret, and trailed by a very reluctant Runt. As usual, Runt carried the pack holding their food and water for the day. It was a relief to see him doing his job again.

It had taken some serious persuading to get Runt to re-join the crew. In the end, Boss had threatened to send Runt's mother a large bill to cover his share of the expenses from this expedition. There was no way Runt could let that happen. His mother barely had enough to cover her own basic living expenses, and Kurt could see how the thought of it almost made Runt burst with shame and guilt. So here he was, back where he belonged. As if he could really go local, anyway, Kurt snorted. City boys belonged in the city, not out here with these inbred hillbillies, gnawing on roots and stuff.

Behind them trooped the Boss, looking burly and stern as always. He had that look on his face that let you know he wasn't putting up with any nonsense. He looked back impatiently every few minutes to see if they'd lost Doc and his crew.

Doc puffed his way up the hills. He wore the most absurd outfit: a pair of stiff shorts with suspenders, a loose cotton button-shirt, all white and fluffy, a safari hat, sandals and knee socks, of all things. Knee socks! Kurt was amazed they still made those things. They ended right below the guy's bare, bony knees, and those knees were going to get eaten by blackflies, but who was he to say anything?

The two assistants struggled along with the ridiculous metal chest. Whatever was in that thing had better be good. It was large enough you could wedge a body into it.

After lots of stopping and starting, they finally made it to the place where they had dug the pit. Kurt and Ferret set to work lining the pit with a large fishing net, heads down, mouths shut tight. Doc sat down on the metal chest, and he was fanning his face with some sort of brochure. There were words blazoned across it:

Rare Hominids of the Andes

A Field Guide by Dr. Ronald Wigglesworth

Well, this was nowhere near the Andes, wherever that was, and that brochure looked pretty thin for a field guide. Kurt figured it was a good thing the fella was just using it as a fan. He supposed it might come in handy for starting a fire, too, if they got lost or stranded out here.

Runt was sitting on the pack, chewing on some kind of dirty plant that he must have grubbed from somewhere. "Get over here, Runt. Grab the end of this rope and take it behind those bushes." He figured he'd better stop calling the guy Grunt, since he was so sensitive about it. Besides, he didn't want to get blamed if Runt ran off again.

The rope was set up to cinch the nets tight, once they'd caught their prey in the trap. All they had to do was cover the pit with leafy branches, then have someone wait behind the bushes to pull the rope at the right time. A flawless plan, he figured, so long as the guy with the rope stayed alert. And so long as the trap worked, and the beast didn't go after the guy instead.

Doc lifted himself creakily off the chest and waved his assistants over. They carried the chest a short distance away and opened it, drawing out an old-fashioned camera, a very large lens, and a tripod. The assistants assembled the thing in some bushes twenty paces away from the hole. When they were done, only the tip of the lens peeked out of the bushes. They drew a couple of large, fuzzy microphones and leggy stands out of the chest and set them up back there as well. Doc and his assistants sat themselves down back there, disappearing into the greenery, presumably to wait for some evidence to show up.

"You take the first turn at the rope," Kurt ordered Runt. "Just don't fall asleep this time. We're going to go look for a better vantage point. We'll be able to see you, so watch yourself." Runt shrugged and settled down into the bushes. Something sure seemed to have changed in that guy. He wasn't nearly as easily cowed as he used to be.

Kurt, Ferret and Boss made their way uphill until they found a good spot where they could view the whole site from above.

All they had to do now was wait. Kurt fiddled with his eWare.

GoldenBoy23 /Hurry up and wait #GreatWhiteHunter/

The battery was still holding, but his juice packs were done now. Might as well send out another micro or two before the thing died, he figured. It was useless for navigation out here, anyway. Now there was a mystery that needed solving. GPS didn't work, and even a compass would go wonky sometimes. Nobody seemed to have an answer for that.

☼

We walked deeper into the hills, crossing several lush, green valleys. Each valley was home to a meandering creek, lined with round pebbles. The moister valleys bore great clumps of willow and alder, and here and there, cow parsnips waved their massive seed-heads. The hillsides bore hazelnut and Saskatoon bushes, in amongst tall stands of aspen, fir and spruce. We stopped from time to time to collect nuts or berries, or to refresh ourselves and refill our water bottles with clear, sweet creek water.

At one of our earlier stops, our hairy friend began to speak. His voice was thick, deep and rough, but to our amazement, we shared a common tongue. He let us know we could call him Saska. Somehow, he already knew my name, and Elena's too. I asked him what he called the squirrel, but he just shook his head. Apparently the squirrel hadn't earned a name of his own yet. Judging by how attached the little rodent seemed to be to Saska, it was probably just a matter of time.

For such a demure fellow, there was no doubt that Saska knew how to get by in the bush. Though we followed the landmarks Nana had given me, it was Saska who showed us the way around swampy areas or through thick brush without getting mired or getting thrown off-course.

In the evening, we reached a valley through which a large creek ran. As Elena and I set up camp, Saska went into the water up to his ankles. Moments later, he came back out, proudly holding a thrashing trout in his large, strong hands. Elena cleaned the fish, and we cooked it over our campfire, the smoky flesh complementing our dinner of flatbread, berries and nuts.

We sat together, enjoying the fire, until we could hardly keep our eyes open. Elena and I settled down under our blanket and tried to get some sleep. We had tired ourselves out with the long hike, and we soon succumbed to the call of our dreams. At the other side of the fire lay Saska, his little squirrel friend burrowed into his thick, bushy mops. The night was wholly silent, and the sky was afire with stars.

When I awoke, there was no sign of Saska. I sat up and looked around, groggily. Elena groaned and pulled the blanket more tightly around her shoulders.

I got up, stretching. Saska's barking laugh drew my eye to the creek, where he was knee-deep in the swift waters, washing himself. The squirrel was dancing along the shoreline. Every now and then, Saska would splash a bit of water towards the squirrel, who would quickly hop out of the way. I grinned, thinking it would be best to leave them at their game. I set to work erasing all traces of our campsite. When Elena rose, we would be ready to go.

Up here, high in the hills, Elena's dreams were rich and magical. She saw Ethan, sleeping out under the stars, the familiar sights of the fish camp around him. She brushed his cheek, and then he was gone.

Now she ran through a valley, following a clear, burbling stream. In the water, she saw flashes of gold.

Then she was high in the mountains. The first snows of autumn were in the air, and the leaves were turning. Looking around, she saw the familiar rolling hills of her homeland, and here and there, tucked into the woods, she could see the curls of wood smoke and peaked roofs that marked tiny villages. Far on the horizon, a deep smudge of bad air stained the sky. A sense of foreboding filled her at the sight.

A blast of cold air on her neck shook her awake. Estella stood beside her, grinning, the blanket in her hands. "Wake up, sleepyhead. It's time to go."

☼

By the time evening rolled around, Kurt's anticipation had dulled into low-grade anxiety. They had seen squirrels, birds, and even a fox today, but there was nothing remotely resembling a sasquatch. Boss was silent, but in a dangerous way. Drips of sweat ran down from his temples, and they drew the thirsty flies to him in swarms.

Even Doc had given up on his hiding place by mid-afternoon; he sat now on some kind of folding chair behind his clump of bushes. He appeared to be swatting at insects with his rolled-up brochure. The research assistants were hunkered down in the bushes behind the camera equipment, sharing strips of some kind of dried fruit or meat. They tossed their wrappers casually on the ground.

Runt and Ferret had spelled one another off with the rope a couple of times. Annoyed at their lack of progress, Kurt decided he'd better take a turn. Who knows, maybe he'd get lucky, and he could take all the credit for their success. He jogged down the path to relieve Ferret. Runt still squatted down there beside the little guy. He was probably just avoiding Boss.

Arriving at the bushes, he waved the two boys off and slithered down on his belly to take the end of the rope. Runt and Ferret reluctantly headed back up the hill to the vantage point.

It seemed like an eternity before a cracking sound came from the woods nearby. Doc had been sitting in his chair with one sandal and knee sock removed, scratching at insect bites. At the sound, the man dropped quickly down into the bushes, disappearing in a puff of dust. Kurt held his breath. His heart was racing now.

A hairy dome appeared over the ridge of the hill, lumbering. It was accompanied by a distinct snuffling noise. Kurt heard the shutter of Doc's camera snap several times. The dome rose, and the huge, hairy face of what was unmistakably a bear came into view. *Oh crud*, Kurt thought. He held himself very still.

The bear snuffled his way into the clearing, edging forward. But instead of heading for the pit, he detoured straight towards the bushes where Doc had hidden with his assistants and all his precious equipment.

It all happened so quickly, Kurt lost track of what was going on. He saw the bear shove its furry snout into the bushes, tipping over the camera, its lens flashing orange with the light from the evening sun. Someone shrieked, and then Doc was hopping in a circle through the clearing, one foot socked and sandaled, the other held up off the ground, bare. The bear was right on his tail, goosing him from behind. And then Doc vanished.

Feeling tension on the rope, Kurt pulled with all his might. "Got him!" The bear was putting up a good fight, roaring and straining against the net. "Help me lift him out, quickly!" Boss, Ferret and Runt came charging down the slope. Boss was shaking his head, angrily. He looked as if he might burst.

"You idiot!" Boss yelled. Kurt looked down into the hole. He hadn't caught the bear at all. Instead, firmly wedged into the trap was the bug-eyed, decrepit-looking form of Doc, arms and legs all askew.

"Ooh, sir, sorry, sir," Kurt mumbled, trying to extract Doc from the net as quickly as possible. Doc's safari hat had fallen into the pit and been trampled flat. There was no sign of the bear.

"What happened? Where did the bear go? I lost sight of him," Kurt breathed.

"He grabbed one of those idiots' snacks and left, that's where he went!" Boss barked. Doc's assistants were looking awfully sheepish. One held the remains of the camera tripod; it was looking rather broken. The giant camera lens had a crack through its glass now, and it was smeared with some sort of dirt or grease.

"Well, at least that camera should be perfect for photographing sasquatches now," Kurt muttered.

Boss smacked the back of his head and pushed him aside. "Get out of here, you idiot. I've got to cut this guy free." He bent and pulled out a buck knife, sliced the net open, then clasped arms with Doc and pulled the top half of his body out of the pit. Doc lay on his belly, gasping, his legs dangling. Several mosquitoes took advantage of the moment to land on his bare ankle. Each one lifted a back leg poshly and they bent forwards to enjoy their meal, heads together. Doc's brochure was a crumpled mess in his right hand.

"Are you alright?" Boss looked green now. He was definitely worried. Doc raised himself up on his elbows, drew his knees under him, and sat up. Coughing up dust, he looked Boss directly in the eye. "You call yourself a bounty hunter? You clearly can't tell a hominid from a caniform. Now get me out of here. Our contract is void!"

11. Lost and found

John sat across from Bushy and watched the fire. Sparks flew and danced, and the embers glowed brightly in the night air.

He had only met his father a few times before, always deep in the wilderness. Each encounter had been quiet, comfortable, and brief. He knew that Bushy would likely be gone by morning. He supposed it was in their solitary nature to enjoy each other's quiet presence for a short time, so different from the constant idle chatter of human companionship.

Bushy's face glowed in the firelight, serene as a monk's. He watched his son contentedly. Each took comfort in knowing that the other was there. All was well in their world.

As the night grew deep, John's eyes became heavy. He settled down before the fire, wrapped in a single woven blanket, and let sleep wash over him.

☼

I climbed yet another rise in these foothills, Elena and Saska on my heels. I set a quick pace this morning, eager to reach our goal. I could see the sharp peaks in the nearest mountains which marked a line to the place where Nana said we'd find Uncle John.

The squirrel was still following us. I had thought they were territorial, but apparently he'd marked Saska as his territory. I wondered how much food he'd hidden in my hairy friend's pelt.

We had also picked up a cheeky camp-robber at our campsite. The mischievous grey bird followed us for a while, alighting on branches in our path then gazing down at us with shiny black eyes as we walked by. Elena pinched off a small piece of flatbread and left it on a stump. After we passed, the bird swooped down to snatch his meal. He left us alone after that.

As we crested the hill, I gasped in shock as a hairy beast barrelled past me, knocking Elena down and leaping on Saska. "No," I yelled, grabbing the beast's hairy back from behind. "Leave him alone!" The squirrel had leaped up a tree, and from that safe vantage point, he scolded us all furiously.

Saska and the beast were trembling, and suddenly I realised they were not fighting at all. They were laughing silently and thumping one another on the back. The squirrel was pelting them both with pine cones from his safe perch.

"Don't do that to me!" I gasped. "You nearly scared me to death." I helped Elena get up. She looked a bit dazed, but she shook herself and began to brush the dust and twigs off her clothes.

Still thumping the huge beast on the back, Saska turned to us, his canines bared in a huge grin. "Bushy," he said. "Grampa."

Grampa? Oh dear.

"I'm Estella," I said pressing a hand to my chest, "and the poor girl who you just trampled is Elena. Would you happen to know our Uncle John? We're looking for him."

Bushy just grinned. When he did that, I sure could see the family resemblance between him and Saska. Bushy was definitely the older of the two, with a wizened face encircled with grizzled hair. Like Saska, he was naked except for a thick, matted pelt of fur. He was easily as tall as Saska, who towered over me, though he wasn't as burly. His body was long, and his legs were relatively short and slightly bowed. His hairy toes were splayed, gripping the shale of the hillside. Despite his apparent advanced age, he still looked strong and wiry.

Jostling one another, Saska and Bushy headed down towards a small clearing, where a thin trail of smoke could be seen winding lazily from the heart of a campfire.

Ronald followed the hapless crew down out of the hills as the sun set. What a useless bunch. He couldn't believe he'd come all the way out here for this. As far as he could tell, they had nothing to show for the time they'd spent out here already.

He knew it was a bit of a gamble trying to catch a sasquatch, but at very least he could have obtained some decent photographs. He'd invested heavily in that high-end equipment which would capture the images in film, the old-fashioned way. Nobody trusted digital imagery anymore; it was just too easy to modify. But now his precious Leica SL-XXII was damaged, his tripod was mangled, and all he'd gained were a few pictures of a bear's dorsal hump. He'd be laughed at by his colleagues if word ever got out.

Then again…. He rubbed his chin whiskers thoughtfully. Why not develop the film and see how the photos look? You never know.

He hiked along behind the bounty hunters, his research assistants still lugging the equipment chest. It was full dark before he realized that they had somehow missed the village.

The sounds of the night closed in around Kurt. An owl hooted, sending shivers down his spine. Surely they would have reached the village by now? He had no idea. There wasn't even a moon to see by.

Kurt had been in the lead, but he hadn't really been paying attention. He was still upset about how the day had gone, and his mind had been wandering. He stopped, pushing Ferret out in front.

"Which way?" he asked Ferret. The little fellow just shrugged and scratched his arms, sniffing.

Kurt let out a deep sigh as the others caught up and gathered around him. "Ferret's gone and gotten us lost. I suggest we spend the night here. It will be easier to find our way in the morning."

Ferret looked surprised, but he didn't say anything. Runt just looked thoughtful.

Boss huffed angrily, but since he had no idea how to get to the village either, he acquiesced. Doc just groaned and shook his head. The research assistants put down the metal chest, sat down beside it huffily, and dug around in their pockets for snacks. It seemed like they were always eating.

We need a fire, Kurt thought. *At least it will keep the beasties away.* "Ferret, Runt, you guys make yourselves useful. Go look for some firewood."

As they turned to go, a low grunt sounded from the bushes. Kurt didn't know what it was, but it sounded large. With a bellow, something big, four-legged and hairy charged towards him. Oh, crud... "Run!"

Everyone scattered.

☼

Ferret scooted up a tree, while the others headed into the bushes in every direction. Runt hunkered down behind a boulder. Whatever the beast was, it was angry. It barrelled through the clearing, into the bushes and away.

"What the bejeezus was that?" Runt heard Ferret ask from his perch in the tree. He cautiously returned to the clearing as the others came back, one by one. There was no sign of the beast.

Unfortunately, there was also no sign of Kurt. Ferret and Runt got a fire going, thinking Kurt would make his way back eventually. The others gathered around a fire. They were hungry, and they hadn't brought anything besides a few snacks with them, as they had planned to be back at the village by nightfall. At least the fire would keep the bugs and the beasties away.

Hours passed, and still there was no sign of Kurt. The others decided to wait until morning, then they could look for him on the way back to the village. Surely they would have heard something if he had been hurt by that moose, or bear, or boar, or rabid donkey, or whatever that creature had been. Runt wrapped his jacket around himself, laid back, and tried to get some sleep.

12. Another kind of treasure

By the time Kurt shook the angry moose off his trail, he was utterly lost. It was pitch black out except for the lazy blinking of fireflies. Crickets or some kind of beetle shrilled in his ears.

"Guys? Hello?" he called in a low voice, but there was no answer. He didn't want to bring anything big and hairy down on himself. He shivered; the night was cool and dew was rising. "Stupid woods," he muttered. He'd rather be in the city any day. The insects paused for a moment in their awful trilling, then resumed.

He decided to wait until dawn. Then he'd have some hope of finding his way out of here. He settled down on a smooth patch of ground, hoping he was well off the trail of any kind of lumbering animal, but determined to stay awake so he didn't become somebody's dinner.

Kurt awoke when the morning sun struck his eyelids, sharp as a knife. He must have dozed off. Blinking and squinting, he pushed himself upright. His whole body ached, and he was stiff from head to toe. He saw ants stumbling in lazy circles around him. They were half red and half black, and the black part was much larger than the red; they were like some sort of cobbled-together mutant. Then he jumped upright in alarm. His clothes were crawling with them, and his skin was on fire.

Hopping madly, Kurt attempted to shake the ants out of his clothes. "I... hate... bitey... things!" Running down slope, he found his way to a little creek, where he quickly stripped and submerged himself. "Take that, you horrible biting monsters!" He watched a few hapless ants swirl their way downstream, their legs struggling helplessly.

Calming himself, he rinsed his button shirt, underwear and trousers, then laid them on a rock beside the creek. He went back into the water and scrubbed everything: his face, his neck, his hair, and every crevasse which might conceal an ant, or even just sweat and grime. The water chilled his thin body, and he was covered with gooseflesh, but it was such a relief to freeze the insect bites that dotted his skin from head to toe.

Looking down into the water, he realised that the rocks looked weird here. A lot of them were some kind of hard white stone, and there were flashes of metal embedded in the stone in a few places. What was that, iron pyrite? He picked up a stone and dug his thumb into the metal. It was soft enough to dent.

No really, he thought..... *Gold?*

Gold!

His face lit up as he realised what he'd just found. Forget the sasquatch, he'd found gold! It was just like the old stories.

Pulling his wet clothes back on, he made a sack out of his undershirt and started loading it up with every shiny rock he could find. He realised he could only carry so much, and he'd have to remember this spot so he could come back.

He pulled his eWare out of his jacket pocket and tried the GPS function, but it located him somewhere in the middle of the Pacific Ocean. Typical. Oh well, he'd find another way to mark the spot. He tapped out a quick micro:

GoldenBoy23 / soaking wet, struck it rich #goldinthewoods/

Then, pausing, he realised another thing. He was going to have to keep this a secret. If Boss found out about the gold, that would be the end of it for Kurt. Guaranteed, Boss would claim the treasure for himself. He hit the delete button on the micro, but not before a reply buzzed through:

Sissy_girl @ GoldenBoy23 / save some for me =D/

He grinned and sent a reply:

GoldenBoy23 @ Sissy_girl /XD/

He sat beside the creek, watching his clothes steam in the morning sun, and started to make a plan.

☼

I walked ahead with Elena. Sure enough, there was Uncle John, sitting before a tiny campfire. He was roasting something unrecognizable on a stick. He didn't look very surprised to see us, though we'd never sought him out here in the wilderness before.

We trotted over and hugged him, both trying to talk at once. "Uncle, we need your…" "You won't believe who we met!"

"Girls, girls, one at a time please. You're making my head spin. What's going on?"

At that moment, as if to defy the need for words of any kind, Saska and

Bushy stepped into sight.

"Ah," John said.

"Ah? Is that all you're going to say? Look who we met!" Elena crowed.

John sighed. "Yes, that's my Papa. And I haven't met the other fellow, but I see a distinct family resemblance."

"What!?" Elena and I both yelled simultaneously.

His Papa? That we hadn't foreseen. I felt like some sort of veil had been torn away from my eyes. All sorts of pieces were falling into place in my mind. Things that hadn't made sense before, like why John was so big and hirsute, when Grampa was a relatively small man without a whole lot of body hair. Things like John's solitary nature, and his habit of spending weeks at a time in the wilderness. Things that Nana had always been so mysterious about; she was very clever at deflecting questions.

My mind raced. Did this mean Elena and I were part sasquatch too? No, it didn't, I concluded. We were related in blood to John on Nana's side only, and she was clearly all human.

While all this was running through my head, John and Saska had greeted one another formally. Elena looked just as disoriented as I felt. I took her hand, as much for my own reassurance as for hers.

By the time we had our heads on straight, Saska and Bushy were heading off into the bush.

"Wait!" I called, "where are you going?"

Saska looked back and met my eyes, but it was John who answered my question.

"Three's a crowd, but for a sasquatch, five's a metropolis. They just need some time alone. They'll be back."

I sighed, then Elena and I turned to Uncle John. He braced himself in preparation for our barrage of questions. But to his surprise, and to our own, the barrage didn't come. Quite honestly, I don't think either of us even knew where to begin. Instead, we slumped down.

"Can we have some breakfast?" Elena asked, meekly. Her stomach growled.

John grinned and tossed her his pack. She rummaged through it hungrily.

☼

Saska followed Bushy for some distance before Bushy stopped and turned to face him. Saska's squirrel friend had burrowed into the hair on the back of his neck, and he had finally stopped scolding Bushy. He peeped out curiously.

"Pretty," he rumbled. Saska just nodded. They turned and continued walking. "Danger in the village," Bushy growled. Saska nodded again. "Make your winter nest here. Nobody will come this far." Saska nodded once more. He fully agreed with Bushy.

"Don't follow the girl." Saska turned to Bushy, puzzled. "Much danger. It will end badly."

"Why?" Saska asked, his furry face scrunched up with puzzlement.

"She needs human company. Loneliness hurts humans. And some humans would like to hurt you. Not safe."

Saska nodded slowly, understanding. He was used to being solitary, but humans lived in tribes. Alone, they would perish from sadness. He remembered how lonely he felt when he first went off on his own. It was that horrible loneliness that had drawn him to Estella in the first place. If it felt that bad to a sasquatch to be alone, it horrified him to think of how it would affect Estella.

Something rustled in the bushes. Bushy reached out with a well-practiced hand, quick as a dart, and snatched up a rabbit. He snapped its neck with a quick jerk, the sudden violence startling the squirrel in Saska's fur. The little fellow chirped angrily, standing up tall on four rigid legs, tufts of Saska's fur clenched in his fists.

"No fear, little one," Bushy grumbled. "I won't eat you."

He proceeded to skin the rabbit with his bare hands as they circled back towards the campfire, the skin and fur coming away in strips. He was happy to have a small gift of food for his son.

Boss dug his boot into Runt's ribs. "Get up!" Runt groaned, rolling away from the offending boot, and pushed himself upright. It was dawn. Doc and the two hapless assistants were stirring, and there was no sign of Kurt. He didn't see Ferret at first, then the little guy came out of the bushes, tucking his shirt into his pants.

Looking around, Runt saw that they were still hopelessly lost. Nothing looked familiar, while at the same time, everything looked the same. Wilderness in every direction. No familiar landmarks. He watched as Ferret carved his tag into the trunk of an aspen tree with his pen knife, a cartoon face with two long slashes like fangs. *Typical city-street boy, has to leave his mark on everything*, Runt thought, rolling his broad shoulders.

The research assistants were sitting up, munching on some sort of processed food, the wrappers crumpled beside them. Doc winced and stretched his creaky limbs. He looked at Boss. "Well, how do we get out of here?" Boss glared at him and turned away, scanning the area.

"East," he decided. "We need to go towards the rising sun. That should take us right back to the village."

Doc pulled out his compass and squinted at it. The needle was twitching, and it wouldn't stabilize in any single direction. Good thing it was a clear day; they could use the sun to navigate.

The not-so-merry adventurers gathered up their gear and began tromping their way eastward, Runt carrying all the bounty hunters' gear on his back as usual, and the two research assistants stumbling along, lugging the ridiculous metal trunk between them.

Realising that he had no idea where he was, Kurt elected to follow the creek downstream. Sooner or later, he knew it would join up with another stream, or even a river. The drop-off point had been beside a river, and that was his ticket out of here.

He tried walking along the shore of the stream, but he soon bogged down in the thick vegetation. Fallen trees blocked his path and brambles scratched him. He found clusters of plump moose droppings which reminded him of chocolate eggs, and he saw some mushrooms of questionable edibility. His stomach rumbled. For once he regretted letting Runt carry everything, as Runt had all their food and water. He wished he'd paid more attention to what the villagers ate. He had no idea what was edible in these woods. He picked a few shiny red berries and tucked them into his jacket pocket, thinking he'd try them if he got desperate enough.

Giving up on the shore, Kurt pulled off his leather boots and tied their laces together. He stuffed his socks inside the boots and rolled up his pant legs. He pulled a plastic bag out of his pocket and tucked his eWare into it, then tied it up tight and put it back in his pocket.

With the boots slung over one shoulder and his undershirt full of gold-laced rocks over the other, he stepped into the stream and started walking along the streambed. At first, his feet were torn and bruised by the rocks, but he stopped noticing once they became numbed by the icy water. He was making good progress, he thought, feeling a sense of accomplishment.

The sun was high in the sky when he decided to take a break. A long, flat rock jutted out into the creek. He set down his boots and sprawled himself on the rock, staring up into the sky. Birds spun and called in the air above him, their feathers bright with sunlight. Flies buzzed here and there. Maybe it was the exercise, and maybe it was the sound of the creek burbling along beside him; something lulled him to sleep.

A loud snuffle woke him. He cracked open his eyes, feeling quite disoriented, and saw a large, hairy snout nosing his jacket. With a yell, he rolled away, and the bear jumped back.

Uh oh...

The bear began to rock back and forth, menacingly. Then suddenly, it charged. Alarmed, Kurt fell back into the water, cracking his head. Everything went black.

13. Tracing circles

Ronald was starting to wonder whether these woods really had it in for him. Boss led the way due east, unerringly, but it was an absurd route. They dared not deviate from their course, in case they became even more lost. This meant they were forced to hike up and down steep ravines, through thickets of prickly bushes, over fallen logs and right through swamps.

Ronald's knees were scabbed, his arms and legs were scratched, and every time they passed through or near any wetlands, he was devoured by mosquitoes and biting flies. While crossing one particularly slippery stream, he very nearly lost his poor Tilley hat. He had accidentally knocked it off his head while swatting at the vicious flies, and it had landed in the water and been sucked under with the current. If it had not snagged on a submerged branch, it would have been lost forever. As it was, he had to lay on the shore on his stomach and reach in to fish it out with his walking stick. The whole experience was quite humiliating.

The only one who seemed to be faring alright was Runt. He'd smeared some sort of grease on his face and hands, and the flies were leaving him alone. He munched on the berries that they found along the way. Ronald didn't dare eat any, since the first ones he'd tried had given him the trots. That was just further proof that these woods didn't want him here, in his opinion.

His assistants looked miserable, but at least they had the sense to keep their mouths shut. They continued lugging the equipment between them, for what it was worth. He really had no use for it now, unless they were to stumble upon a sasquatch or some other sort of rare beast. Even if they did, he was pretty sure his camera lens was so badly damaged that it wouldn't take any useable pictures.

Ronald looked ahead and saw that Boss had called the troupe to a halt. He scrambled over to the aspen grove where the others waited. Ferret was studying something on the side of the tree. Boss was looking at it too; he had gone very red in the face. Was the exertion too much for the man? Ronald took a swig of water from his bottle, then he nearly choked as he saw what Ferret had found. There was the mark that Ferret had made this morning, carved neatly into the bark of the tree.

They had gone in a full circle.

☼

"So," I began, looking across at Uncle John. We'd boiled a pot of water over the fire, and John, Elena and I now each held a steaming mug of tea made from some wild mint that we'd picked beside the stream that burbled nearby.

John raised one of his impressive, bushy eyebrows at me.

"Bushy's really your father," I stated, my voice flat. John nodded. "So are sasquatches just big, hairy people then?"

He shook his head. "I think we have lived separately for thousands of years, long enough to be counted as different species. But as you can see, we aren't that different, since we can successfully reproduce together."

I remembered the things Grandpa had taught us when we were little about how different species originated. He'd told us a story about some little birds that lived in isolation on a bunch of islands, and how their isolation let them evolve into different species. Their colours, songs, eating and nesting habits all became unique over time.

Sasquatches seemed to be pretty rare, so I wondered how they had survived as a species for this long. There must be a lot of inbreeding, I thought.

"How are they different from us?" Elena asked, her hands wrapped firmly around her mug. The steam rose in front of her face and seemed to swirl before it disappeared above her.

"Well, let's see. They are solitary, where we are social. They are of the earth, whereas we are of the mind. You know all those things we do at the village to try and get closer to nature? When we sleep out under the stars, or eat exclusively from the wilds, or make our clothes and tools out of what nature provides?" Elena and I nodded. "Those things are naturally part of the sasquatch. They are inside him, innately. He doesn't have to try and get closer to nature, because nature is within him. For us, it's more of an effort."

Elena looked puzzled, but somehow it all made sense to me. In a sense, our whole way of life in the village was a construct. Nana had explained to me how our grandparents' generation had set it up deliberately, creating an ideal nature-based society with minimal impact on the world around us. It was a conscious reversal of industrialization, and a way of spitting in the face of the urban powers. These weren't the general teachings that the village children were exposed to, but Nana had explained many things to me while she taught me how to weave.

I reached over and squeezed Elena's arm with a reassuring glance. I'd explain it later, the look said. She nodded slowly.

"In what other ways are we different?" I asked. "I can see that they are bigger and hairier than us, and they are not as socially oriented. Is there anything else?"

"They are without guile," John explained. "Humans will sell each other out at the drop of a hat. You won't see that in the village, but that's because it's been consciously removed from our social order by our elders. But look at the bounty hunters."

Ah, I thought. They were pretty awful to one another. That poor boy, Runt, especially seemed to get kicked around a lot. I'd wondered about that.

"Sasquatches have no capacity for betrayal. They are as authentic as you can get."

With a shuffle of shale beneath their feet, Bushy and Saska announced their return. Bushy held what appeared to be a skinned rabbit by the hind feet, and the little squirrel was perched atop Saska's head, looking outraged. Bushy handed the rabbit to John, who grinned, spitted it and set it over the coals to roast. My stomach turned over. I was alright with fish, but I would never make a good carnivore. I glanced at Elena; she looked pale.

Saska settled beside me and brushed my arm with his huge hand. I grinned at him and took his hairy fingers in both my hands, studying them. The pelt on them was glorious and thick, and only the strong, flat nails and sturdy knuckles stood out, hairless. I stroked his fingers, curiously.

The little squirrel edged down Saska's arm towards my hands. He moved in sudden jerks, staying completely still between movements, as if that would make him invisible. I giggled, and he darted back up onto Saska's neck, but his little face peeked out at me, his shiny black eyes unblinking. I pulled a bit of flatbread out of my pack and held it out to him. He edged forward cautiously, then he snatched it and disappeared onto Saska's far shoulder with his treat.

"Shifty, that would be a good name for you. Or Twitchy. Yes, definitely Twitchy," I said softly as he shook himself then scratched rapidly behind his ear with one of his long-nailed hind feet.

Saska hummed gently and leaned in a little closer to me. Elena watched us, curiously, as Bushy and John hunkered over the spitted rabbit. Bushy had picked a few needles off a juniper bush and he was sprinkling them over the rabbit. They sizzled and released a pungent scent.

Though it was mid-day, the air was still cool at this elevation. "Snow is coming soon," John reflected. "We will have to get your girls back to the village before it does. Some of these valleys will become difficult to travel through."

"Can we stay for a few days?" I begged. I felt so good inside, so peaceful and nourished by the mountain air. But I knew that John had come here to be alone.

"Today and tomorrow would be okay. Then we need to get you back home. I'll walk back with you. You've accomplished what you came for, no? Your friend will be safe here now."

Sadly, I looked up at Saska. His big hand was still cradled in my smaller ones, and it radiated warmth. I traced circles on his huge palm. His deep brown eyes met mine and he rumbled softly, deep in his chest, as if to say, all will be well.

14. The way home

The sound of sloshing water slowly brought Kurt around. He groaned and opened his eyes. A flash of pain ran through his head, and he winced. He could feel cold water lapping against his legs. The sun was setting behind the trees. He bent over and coughed, curling himself into a ball. Everything went dark again.

A ray of light in his eyes tore him from sleep. It was a new day. His head thrummed in agony. Shading his eyes, he looked out at the water before him. This was no little creek; he must have been washed downstream into the river. Disbelieving, he watched his eWare bob past in its plastic bag, drifting on the current like a jellyfish. He looked around him, then groaned. There was no sign of his stash of gold; he must have lost it when the bear charged him. His boots were gone, too.

He pushed himself to his feet, painfully. He felt as if he'd been run over. His head pounded loudly now, and when he felt the back of his scalp, he found a soft, tender, raised bump.

Looking up the bank, he was surprised to find that he knew this place. There was the circle of grass that marked the drop-off point. How many days had it been since they arrived? He couldn't remember. Anyway, all he had to do was wait. Sooner or later, the chopper would come to collect him.

☼

Boss and his hapless entourage were so discouraged by their lack of progress, they elected to spent the night in the aspen grove. How could the sun have led them astray? Boss couldn't figure it out. He'd have to think of another way to chart their course the next day.

In the end, it was Runt who proposed a workable solution. Why not find a creek, then trace its route down to the river? Once they found the river, they would be able to locate the drop-off point where the chopper would collect them.

So began a day's soggy march. Locating a creek was not that difficult to do; navigating it was another matter. The troupe slipped, stumbled and slid their way through the icy water, having found the bushes largely impassable. Doc's assistants seemed relieved to discover that the metal chest floated. They let it bob along between them, holding loosely onto its handles, using its top as a table for their snacks.

At least the water was clear and safe to drink, so nobody suffered from thirst. In Runt's opinion, it was probably a good thing that Doc's scabbed knees were getting thoroughly washed, since it would help prevent infection. Also, the flies weren't as bad in the creek. They didn't seem to bother him, but some of the others had been eaten alive the day before.

Spotting a cluster of high-bush cranberries littered with fruit, Runt led the troupe out of the creek for a break. They stuffed themselves with the tart berries, though for some reason Doc chose to abstain. He just laid flat on his back, dripping into the forest soil, his hat over his eyes.

It was early evening when they heard the roar of the river. Disbelieving, Runt realised he could hear the low thrum of a chopper over the sound of the water.

Dropping his walking stick, Doc charged up the shale hillside and leaped up onto the ridge, his skinny arms waving frantically, the silhouette of his knobby knees bobbing. Runt grinned at Ferret and they set off after the old man. Who knew he could move so quickly?

☼

Those two days in the wilderness were among the most memorable moments so far in my young life.

Bushy came and went; he seemed uncomfortable being around so many people at once. He was sweet and wise, not unlike my old Grandpa in many ways. It was so easy to see the similarities between the sasquatches and us. They seemed to reflect our better qualities, while they had none of the unpleasant ones.

Elena spent much of her time talking to Uncle John, seeking answers to her many questions. She literally went about wide-eyed like she was seeing things for the first time. I knew the feeling. I felt like my whole reality had shifted, and nothing was as it had seemed.

I was revelling in Saska's company. Much of our time was spent together in silence, just enjoying the world around us. I put a few corn-rows into his magnificent hair, teasing out the burrs and tangles. He touched my arm from time to time, as if reassuring himself that I was really there. Even Twitchy was getting used to me; he had stopped scolding me whenever I got close, and instead gazed at me hopefully with his bright, black eyes. It probably didn't hurt that I'd been giving him little treats at every opportunity.

At night, Elena and I curled under our blanket to keep warm, and Saska slept on my other side, the curve of his warm back pressed against mine. I slept deeply, without dreaming, and I woke feeling wholly refreshed.

☼

I woke just before dawn after our second night there. Everything was still. The sky behind the mountains was black, but towards the valleys, it was beginning to glow. Several ravens flew over, calling out their morning thoughts softly to one another.

My feeling of peace was mingled with a sense of loss, because I knew that Elena and I would have to start back for the village this morning.

The others rose soon after me, limbs stretching and joints cracking. Elena, John and I gathered our things, and I turned to face Saska. Our eyes met, and impulsively, I pushed our blanket into his hands. It was one of the first ones I'd ever woven with Nana, and it was simple work, but solid. I'd even worked a few little charms of protection into the pattern, just as Nana had taught me.

"Be safe, be warm," I murmured to him.

Twitchy, peeking out of Saska's hair, turned his head a little to the side, quizzically. Saska reached out a hand and brushed my cheek lightly. Then he wrapped the blanket around his massive shoulders and turned to go.

My heart heavy, I followed Elena and Uncle John down out of the hills. I had so much to think about, I hardly even noticed where we were going. It was a good thing John was in the lead.

Our final night in the wilderness, I missed that blanket, but just a little. It pleased me to think of Saska and Twitchy, out there somewhere wrapped in my blanket. John shared his blanket with me and Elena, and it was a small for the three of us, but our shared body heat kept off the night's chill. By the following evening, we were home.

☼

Back at the village, my first stop was Nana's cabin. I found her sitting on the porch, mending nets. I was all set to bombard her with questions: why didn't you tell me about Uncle John? Why, how, how could you just let Bushy go and never see him again? But she met my eyes, and I saw in her deep gaze both understanding and deep compassion. As I fell into her embrace, my tears started to flow hotly.

"I know, girl," she crooned, rubbing my back, "I know."

I took a deep breath, sniffled, and rubbed my face. Then I picked up a net and sat beside her to help with the mending. My questions had dissolved.

Epilogue

The winter was harsher than some, but no longer than most. As is often the way of seasons, spring came suddenly upon the village, and the sun finally had some real warmth to it, so unlike the weak rays of winter. The snow melted rapidly, and the woods filled with birdsong.

There were a few days of mud, but it wasn't long before the trails had cleared and the villagers shifted into the regular activities of spring and summer.

One sunny day, Ethan spotted a lone hiker atop a ridge overlooking the village. It appeared to be a robustly built man, carrying a large backpack, a sturdy walking stick in his hand. The man began to pick his way carefully down the hill.

Slowly, Ethan began walking towards the man, but then in sudden recognition, he picked up his pace. Soon they were pounding one another on the back, grinning.

"Runt, you came back!"

The man coughed into his hand, then looked at Ethan sidelong. "If it's alright with you…"

"Yes?" Ethan encouraged.

"I'd like to stay."

Ethan grinned. "Well, we could always use another pair of hands to gut the fish!"

Runt groaned and rolled his eyes, and Ethan elbowed him lightly in the ribs, teasingly, then threw an arm over his shoulders and walked with him down to the village. Runt sighed, happily. For some things, it's worth gutting a few fish.

☼

As soon as the mountain trails were clear, I threw some things into a bag and headed out. It was early yet for travel, but I couldn't wait any longer. I had to go!

I retraced the path that Elena and I had taken last autumn, up through the hills towards the mountains. Deer and moose had kept the trail open, and here and there, I could see where they had nibbled the bark from the willows that had fed them all winter. I picked my way over the streams, their waters swollen now with snowmelt. The water tasted of ice, grit and winter sun.

By the second evening, I found the place where we had met up with Uncle John last autumn. Some leaves and litter had fallen into his old fire pit. I cleaned it out and soon got a little fire going with my flint.

I was bent over the fire, blowing life into the flames, when a faint cough sounded behind me letting me know that I had company. I stood, not looking yet, savouring the moment. A huge, hairy arm slid around my waist, and I turned slowly, grinning. Saska's huge brown eyes met mine, the message in them plain to see. I had found my way home.